The Colloc

GUIDO GOZZANO

THE COLLOQUIES
and selected letters
translated by J.G. Nichols

CARCANET

First published in 1987 by
CARCANET PRESS LIMITED
208-212 Corn Exchange, Manchester M4 3BQ UK
and
198 Sixth Avenue, New York, NY 10013 USA

British Library Cataloguing in Publication Data

Gozzano, Guido
    The colloquies and selected letters.
    I. Title. II. I colloqui. *English*
    851'.912 PQ4817.09

    ISBN 0-85635-628-X

The Publisher acknowledges financial assistance from the
Arts Council of Great Britain.

Typeset in 10pt Palatino by Bryan Williamson, Manchester
Printed in England by SRP Ltd, Exeter

Contents

Acknowledgements

In translating *I colloqui* I have worked from Giorgio Bàrberi Squarotti's *Guido Gozzano. Poesie* (Rizzoli, Milan, 1977), with occasional reference to the editions by Edoardo Sanguineti (Einaudi, Turin, 1973, third edition) and Andrea Rocca (Mondadori, Milan, 1983, second edition); for "La signorina Felicita" I also used the edition by Edoardo Esposito (il Saggiatore, Milan, 1983).

In selecting from and translating the letters I have used Alberto De Marchi's *Poesie e prose di Guido Gozzano* (Garzanti, Milan, edition of 1961, reprinted 1978). Asterisks are used to indicate passages which I have omitted from the letters.

I am grateful to: Michael Schmidt for his advice in planning this volume; to Joseph Griffiths and Terence Pey for comment on the verse translations; to Anna Maria Jubb for her meticulous and helpful comparison of my translation of the letters with the originals.

Introduction

I too was from another century

IN 1907, with the publication of *The way of refuge* (*La via del rifugio*), Guido Gozzano strolled into prominence (in Montale's admiring phrase) "in a friendly way, with his hands in his pockets". Four years later a second volume of poems, *The colloquies* (*I colloqui*), increased his reputation. Today several good editions of his poems are in print, and the critical work grows steadily. He wrote much fascinating prose, and indeed much verse that he never published in book form; but today it is *The colloquies* which receive, quite rightly, the most, the most appreciative, attention.

In England he is still virtually unknown. A reader coming to *The colloquies* for the first time, and noticing that more than half of Gozzano's short life was lived in the last century, may well wonder where his work belongs. With the second half of the nineteenth century, dominated poetically by Carducci? Or with the modernists of this century? When he has finished the poems the reader is likely to be left still wondering.

There are obvious traditional qualities. The poems are discursive and expansive. Gozzano works, not by a rapid succession of stabs at meaning, or by a piling-up of images with no apparent connection, but very simply and straightforwardly, in a rather leisurely way. Syntax, so far from being fractured, is not even bruised. In poem after poem the theme is announced:

> Sadness, sweet thing, you used to be the friend,
> not long since, of the boy just back from school...
> ("The ultimate infidelity")

> I, once upon a time, was Paul. The name
> Virginia stirs me still...
> ("Paul and Virginia")

> How often in bright lands among bright flowers,
> on shipboard, near the rigging, have my dreams
> been only of your snows and sombre limes...
> ("Turin")

Then the theme is developed at what is often, for a modern poem, quite some length. Finally the poem is rounded off neatly:

> Oh, honestly I don't know what
> 's more sad than never to be sad again.
> ("The ultimate infidelity")

Have mercy, lovers! Hear
my prayer! Mercy on this ironical
desert of mine where such chimeras are!
("Paul and Virginia")

No point in getting roused... I do agree,
my wise Gianduia, Piedmont's puppet-clown!...
("Turin")

Much of the poetry is quit᠅ clearly narrative. This includes the
very best poems – "Paul and Virginia" and especially "La signorina
Felicita" – and it is significant that these two best poems are also
the longest. Another narrative, "Wintry", might even have been
written, although with some loss of élan, in prose as an old-
fashioned short story, one with a shock O. Henry ending.

With this expansiveness, this willingness to explain, goes a
remarkable clarity, and clarity is not the most striking feature of
modernist poetry, in Italy or anywhere else. The references and
allusions Gozzano makes are far from esoteric: he clearly expects
his reader not only to catch them, but to catch them without
feeling particularly clever. Even those which might cause some
difficulty to an English reader are not hermetic: an Italian reader
would usually have no problem. To take a few examples: the
epigraph to the first section of *The colloquies*, "The youthful error",
is very familiar to Italians as a quotation from the first sonnet of
Petrarch's *Canzoniere*; Bernardin de Saint-Pierre's *Paul et Virginie*,
on which "Paul and Virginia" is based, is the book "which made
all the world weep"; then "Jacopo's fate, so sad, in Foscolo's
tender book", which is mentioned in "The friend of Grandmother
Speranza", alludes to the famous *Last letters of Jacopo Ortis*, a work
which performed the same service, or disservice, for Italian youth
at the turn of the eighteenth and nineteenth centuries as, a quarter
of a century before, had been performed for a whole European
generation by another work mentioned more than once in the
same poem – *The sorrows of young Werther*. Even when Gozzano
refers to people only by their first names, it is not in order to be
evasive or oblique, but only to show a rather insouciant familiar-
ity. The "Giacomo" mentioned in "Turin" is Leopardi, and
Gozzano makes the matter more than clear by quoting, within
inverted commas, from two of Leopardi's poems. In the second
poem entitled "The colloquies", the one which concludes the
volume, "Artur" is certainly more obscure than anything so far,
but his identification with Schopenhauer is helped by the colloca-
tion with "Friedrich" who cannot be anyone else but Friedrich
Nietzsche, who is not only mentioned, but also used as a rhyme-

word, several other times in *The colloquies*. Even "Makakita, his one friend" of "In the survivor's home" – who might at first seem to be as exotically elusive as Eliot's Pipit, Hakagawa, or Mr Silvero – has been introduced to us in an earlier poem as "an ape called Makakita": Totò Merùmeni has some strange friends, it is true, but we do know who they are. There is something reassuring about such a sphere of reference, and the reader never feels that he is trying, and failing perhaps, to break into a social circle which would prefer to exclude him.

Something else which distinguishes Gozzano from modernist poets is his faithfulness to traditional verse-forms. This must have been the result of a conscious decision; it cannot have been simply that the option of free verse did not occur to him: he had read much French poetry in irregular verse, and other Italian poets of his time were experimenting with it, including the great d'Annunzio. Why then did Gozzano make such a decision? Would it not seem to be the obvious thing to loosen the verse up in keeping with his choice of a humdrum, domestic subject matter? Perhaps, but for the moment we may notice that his insistence on writing of little, ordinary things is matched by his insistence on the poem as a highly-wrought artefact. Quite alien to Gozzano are both the sentiment and the looseness of form in Sergio Corazzini's famous cry:

> Why do you call me a poet?
> I am not a poet.
> I am only a little lad who is weeping.
> ("Desolation of the poor sentimental poet", 1906)

Gozzano was made, not only of sterner, but more meticulous stuff.

Like many another poet, Gozzano has suffered the misfortune of having a label pasted over his contents. The fact that he shares the label with, among others, Corazzini should make us suspicious of its accuracy. Gozzano is often included among the "crepuscolari" (twilight poets). The term was first used by G.A. Borgese in 1910 with reference to Gozzano's friend, Marino Moretti. In the way in which it is often used now, and in what is probably its most obvious significance, this term has little bearing on the hard, clear outlines of Gozzano's poetry; but in its original intention there is some insight. Borgese compared the history of Italian poetry to a day, of which the second half of the nineteenth century was the twilight, the decline, the decadence. To see Gozzano as in some sense an epigone is not to misread him, and indeed he went to considerable trouble to stress his own dependence on what had gone before. Certainly Borgese's label puts him firmly in the nineteenth century.

And yet, and yet... When we know that a card-carrying modernist like Eugenio Montale has praised Gozzano (and praised him by implication as his own predecessor) then we know that we must think again.

The true child of our times

Anyone who is reading this introduction after reading the poems (introductions seldom introduce) may find himself stirring uneasily at this point. Even if he admits the justice of what has so far been suggested, he may be unable to get out of his head his first impression that Gozzano is very reminiscent of the early T.S. Eliot. Parallels can easily be adduced:

> I'm twenty-five now! Yesterday I wasn't.
> Now I am old. My youth, now it has gone,
> leaves me the present of not being present.

and

> I grow old... I grow old...
> I shall wear the bottoms of my trousers rolled.

The epigraph to the first section of *The colloquies*, "The youthful error", is used for a purpose that Eliot also often had in mind – to contrast the heroic or sublime connotations of the quotation sharply with the mundane matter of the poem. In Gozzano's epigraph Petrarch is brought to mind, to contrast his passionate love of twenty-one years with the inability of Gozzano's protagonist even to love at all. The date which Felicita writes upon the wall, "*September the thirtieth, nineteen-o-seven*", may easily remind us of the dates which Petrarch included in his poems in order to stress the duration of his love for Laura. Apart from that, the incident in Gozzano is immediately qualified by the bathos of

> I didn't smile. Deep down inside I even
> enjoy romantic gestures straight from school.

And that is very like Eliot's

> I smile, of course,
> And go on drinking tea.

Eliot and Gozzano had not read each other, and there is no question of direct influence. What we have is an interesting manifestation of the Zeitgeist: Gozzano is clearly seen to resemble in important ways the poet who introduced modernism into England.

As again with Eliot, we cannot discuss Gozzano for long without mentioning his irony. Its most obvious function is to guard against sentimentality, or at least qualify the sentimentality once it appears:

> A lunar kiss, where clouds are brightening up,
> such as was à la mode some seventy
> years back!

It also has a wider function, in that it distances the speaker from what he is describing, and so underlines his half-humorous, wholly sad, detachment from the life around him:

> But now the Storm is rising on the sea,
> a very beautiful and stylised storm
> as shown in ancient paintings of the Flood.

Most important of all, the irony often consists in a sense, diffused throughout *The colloquies*, that everything is open to mockery:

> Towards nine or so there would assemble there,
> for cards, the entire illustrious faculty
> of local statesmen, viz. the Notary
> Public, the Doctor, and the honoured Mayor;
> but – since I was an absentminded player –
> those gentlemen did not think much of me...
>
> I found things were much pleasanter and cleaner
> among the brightly-coloured crockery...

Modernist poetry in England began with Imagism, and it has continued with images and still more images: the concrete is approved, the abstract frowned upon. The same tendencies are noticeable in Italian poetry. For all the value of Gozzano's discursiveness – and it is worth pointing out that, whatever the current fashion or our personal likes and dislikes, language has to move continually between both the concrete and the abstract, simply because that is how the human mind works – his least successful passages are those where abstract explanation is predominant, his most successful those which consist of sharp, usually visual, images.

> Look at your friends. How they already place
> their diverse faith in diverse schools of thought.
> Not you. You sneer. Now what does your grimace

11

offer the anguished soul? What goal? What butt?
The Homeland? God? Humanity? Words that
the rhetoricians have made nauseous!...

That passage not only suggests the crisis of language and belief that lies behind modernist poetry, but – in its lack of particularity – it illustrates the very faults that modernists try to avoid. Gozzano is most successful when he allows the abstract meaning to emerge of its own accord from the concrete particulars, when he does not have to drag it out by the scruff of its neck. We remember all the "good things in the worst of taste" mentioned so lovingly and so memorably at the beginning of "The friend of Grandmother Speranza" and, among so many other instances, we remember the descriptions of the Vill'Amarena in "La signorina Felicita":

Sad uninhabited fine edifice!
Big-bellied gratings rust away and writhe!
Silence and stealth of rooms! Nothing alive!
An odour of the past pervades the house!
An odour of abandoned emptiness!
Legends are fading on the architrave!

Gozzano frequently works, in what seems to be an authentic modernist way, by a piling-up of disparate images:

Echoes prolong each footstep as it goes
among such odds and ends of time gone by,
and the Marchesa with the Grecian nose,
high-waisted, seen beneath a pagan sky
one bare foot in her hand, takes her repose
umbrageous in a grot of Arcady.

About her, smiling in her Grecian dress
and Grecian dream, who came to die of hunger,
there lay a tattered and promiscuous race:
some furniture, some oil lamps, the odd hamper,
mattresses, rats' nests, crockery: the lumber
that since it is rejected charms my Muse!

Here, however, there is a qualification to be made. We never see in Gozzano the true "musée imaginaire" of modern art with

every clime and age
Jumbled together

for these images do not merely come together in the poet's mind: they are quite naturally and realistically found together in an attic, whatever they may suggest also or symbolise.

12

So it is quite possible – and in surveys of the history of modern Italian poetry almost inevitable – to see Gozzano as a poet who tried to be a modernist and almost succeeded. Yet that judgement may obscure a more important fact. It is not just the nineteenth-century expansiveness we admire, nor just the twentieth-century irony and image-making, but rather the fact that they are found together under the same roof: and this is only one of many contrasts.

The poems show, not so much shock-tactics, as a total strategy of shock and contrast. There is a contrast between the stylised expression, insistently literary and in the strictest of verse-forms, and the domestic and humdrum nature of the content. This is particularly obvious where the contrast between life and art is itself the subject:

> What blessed spells of idleness, at noon
> in the ancestral park where some slight trace
> still lingered of the epoch that had gone!
> The Seasons – armless, broken-nosed, of course,
> knee-deep in dung and grapeskins – nonetheless
> looked over leeks and lettuce in disdain.

There is a related contrast between the past and the present – the present seen through the literary and artistic spectacles of the past, the past seen with the loving but judging eyes of the present. The movement most typical of a Gozzano poem – found in "Paul and Virginia", "La signorina Felicita", and "The friend of Grandmother Speranza" – is from the present to the past and then back again to the present. Characters in the poems are often sharply contrasted: a poet-lawyer and a simple country girl; a middle-aged woman and one who is scarcely more than a child; an innocent little boy and a cocotte. This constant use of glaring contrasts is the main reason why I hesitate to describe Gozzano as a "crepuscolare": of no poet could it less helpfully be said that

> A common greyness silvers everything, –
> All in a twilight...

In his poetry nothing is ever simply itself but always at the same time something else:

> Then came the time for parting; truly bitter
> that parting from another century:
> ladies in crinolines, each hair in order,

13

> leaned out of gardens that appeal to me
> and, sobbing very loudly, waved goodbye
> to diligences making for the border...

The poet sees the present in terms of the past, he uses the present to project himself into the past, and – most important – he sees present and past together in all their disparity.

In *The colloquies* the past is bound to send continual shockwaves through the present, since the poems are full of echoes of previous poets, particularly Dante and Petrarch. There is nothing accidental about this: Gozzano kept notebooks in which he entered the passages he intended to use. He does not try to disguise his borrowings – he flaunts them. Where it is possible that an Italian might not catch the echo, then Gozzano uses inverted commas:

> Midnight was striking loud and long and high
> through that dear region which I do not name.
> I saw the moon above the bell-tower gleam
> out "like a dot upon a massive i".

De Musset is hardly an obscure poet, but Gozzano is taking no chances. Then the allusion may not always be specific, but it is always made obvious that there is an allusion:

> I wandered all around with my regret...
> and lingered by the cemetery-gate
> as people do in books of poetry.

How can we define the effect of this? It is as though the protagonist of the poems, wandering through life with little but literature to guide him (and perhaps rather too much of that), is again and again surprised to find that life really is like literature: his map was right after all. Such passages give us a pleasing gentle shock, for what we have is a reversal of the usual process by which literature is praised for being like life. Gozzano had, in Italian translation, read Oscar Wilde's "The Decay of Lying":

> At twilight nature becomes a wonderfully suggestive
> effect, and is not without loveliness, though
> perhaps its chief use is to illustrate quotations
> from the poets.

In both writers, with humour predominating in Wilde and sadness and alienation in Gozzano, there is a shrewd point behind the dandyish affectation: to our perception, if not in objective reality, nature does, as Wilde insists, imitate art:

14

Where, if not from the Impressionists, do we get
those wonderful brown fogs that come creeping down
our streets, blurring the gas-lamps and changing
the houses into monstrous shadows?... The extraordinary
change that has taken place in the climate of London
during the last ten years is entirely due to a
particular school of Art.

The world of Gozzano's art is a solid and substantial one. This is largely because, while the constituents of this world often clash with each other, they do not fight to a finish. Nothing is there simply to be denigrated, but to enhance something else and in its turn to be enhanced. In the Vill'Amarena we see, above an architrave,

> the flying Daphne as the god draws near
> transmuted into laurel, green for ever...

Then in the drawing-room we see

> tucked inside a looking-glass la Belle
> Otero on a postcard...

Both images are striking; but more striking than either separately is their collocation.

The man I never am, but feign to be!

What is the relation between Gozzano and the protagonist of his poems? The question is bound to arise, whatever artistic distortion we allow for, simply because the two clearly have so much in common. Against a background familiar to Gozzano – the famous park in Turin, the Valentino, for instance, or the Canavese with the town of Ivrea and the River Dora – we see a protagonist who is a poet, and a tubercular one too, with an interest in insects, especially butterflies, and seen sometimes with a woman reminiscent of Amalia Guglielminetti to whom so many of the letters are addressed.

One reason – though certainly not the only reason – for including a selection from the letters in this book is to give some idea of the background to the poems. The letters serve this purpose very well, and the reader is likely to find himself moving back and forth between the poems and the letters. Indeed, the letters are so convenient for this purpose that it is almost as if Gozzano realised... Which brings us to the other reason for including the letters: they are so well written. The portraits of Amalia and

Gozzano which emerge from the letters are effective because they are the result of an artistic effort which, in its slighter way, is comparable to that which gave us the poems. We have, in the letters, not so much the raw material of the poems as similar material shaped in a rather different way.

An autobiographical approach to the poems can at times be misleading or reductive. We have to allow for a certain licence, as when the protagonist (as in "La signorina Felicita") is a lawyer, while Gozzano himself never managed to qualify. Then there seems no doubt, for instance, that the "almighty youngster, square-shouldered, broad of chest" of "Survival of the fittest" is Guido's younger brother, Renato, and the speaker of the poem, who is dying, is readily identifiable with Guido himself. However, the poem is quite clear without any such information, and its significance is wider than such a narrow reading might suggest.

What matters most is that Gozzano is so often at pains both to identify his protagonist with himself and at the same time distinguish his protagonist from himself: with his usual engaging frankness, he tells us that a kind of alter ego is involved. That is why his irony and detachment are so thorough-going: they are not merely stylistic features but symptoms of the deepest psychology of the poems: "I have to smile to see myself alive." The detachment is such that the poems sometimes move between the first person and the third:

> These *Colloquies*... Now sound of body and mind,
> he groups his verses and he alters them,
> weighing the manuscript with even hand.

> – A bit of fun with syllables and rhyme:
> is this what stays of my so fleeting spring?
> Is it all really here, my youthful prime?

The villa appears to be taken from certain verses of mine

Il Meleto, the villa where Gozzano spent so much of his time and which was one of the sources for the Vill'Amarena, has of recent years been carefully restored, furnished with relics of the poet, and opened to visitors. It is easy to see how the poetry could inspire such a proceeding; but it would be a mistake to read the poetry merely (or mainly) in order to gain a picture of life in Turin and its environs in the early years of this century along with a realistic portrait of its inhabitants. No, *The colloquies* form their own world, a world of words which – while they must, as words

16

always must, refer to matters outside themselves – also refer continually, and very interestingly, to each other.

The opening poem of the book not only has the same title as the book, but also has the book for its theme, as does the concluding poem, which repeats the title once more; the protagonist of "In the survivor's home" is identified with Totò Merùmeni; lines from "In the survivor's home" are used as the epigraph to the first poem of the book, and referred to again at the end of "Banquet"; "Paul and Virginia" quotes itself for epigraph; and we could go on and on. The result is such an artistic coherence that – whatever Gozzano was "really" like – he has achieved his aim:

> As for my image, I want it to stay
> twenty, as in a portrait, never altered...

He has made himself like one of his favourite old prints:

> The silent poet hardly glances up,
> happy to find himself in such a group
> with all the sadness of an old engraving.

This self-consciousness, self-obsession, self-quotation may at times be rather precious: one can see the force of Amalia Guglielminetti's shrewd comment on "Paul and Virginia": "...that poem is written with the most subtle artistry, which scholars will certainly enjoy; but it is a virtuoso performance, and it has the coldness of mere virtuosity." One can see the force of this and still believe that "Paul and Virginia" is the best of the poems after "La signorina Felicita". To those who argue that poetry's prime function is to communicate experience of life one can reply that literature and art are a part of life, and – in these poems – the ostentatious literariness and artiness of the protagonist are an important, and attractive, feature of the portrait of him which the book as a whole presents:

> But now the Storm is rising on the sea,
> a very beautiful and stylised storm
> as shown in ancient paintings of the Flood.

Memories are important in *The colloquies*. Often the things remembered are themselves reminiscent of something else, so that the reader – who, after all, is now as distant in time from Gozzano as he was from Carlotta or Speranza or Massimo d'Azeglio – feels he is being moved further and further into the past:

> You seemed a lady weeping, in some frantic
> lyric of Prati's, someone on his way
> to undiscovered isles in the Atlantic...

To balance Amalia Guglielminetti's strictures on "Paul and Virginia" it may be pointed out that nostalgia – the attraction of what is either temporally or spatially out of reach – is at the heart of Gozzano's poetry, and nostalgia always has a wide appeal.

There is a complication. What is offered here is not Gozzano, after all, but a version of him in English. The value of this version is for others to judge; but I must – in order to avoid misunderstanding – draw attention to just one feature of it. The many echoes of English poets are not inadvertent; nor are they there because Gozzano echoed English poets: they are intended to give an effect analogous to the highly literary and allusive language of Gozzano, and they may tease the reader a little if he finds some phrases familiar without at first being able to place them. Some such complications cannot perhaps be avoided; nor indeed did I wish to avoid them. Complications may co-exist with a broad, very human, appeal, as when we have an English version of Gozzano's Italian version of Saint-Pierre's French version of the eternal and international lament for lost innocence:

> Clear from the misty past I see arise
> the land of lost content,
> the land I never knew, and recognise...

Chronology

1883

Guido Gozzano born in Turin, the fourth child of Fausto and Diodata (née Mautino).

His mother's father a friend of Massimo d'Azeglio (1798-1866) and of Cavour (1810-1861).

Both Guido's parents are from Agliè Canavese where their families own the villas – including Il Meleto – which, in various forms, are to figure in his poetry and eventually become the Vill'Amarena of "La signorina Felicita".

1884

Guido baptised. His godmother is Adele Testa, to whom one of his last letters will be written.

1904

Enrols in the Faculty of Law at the University of Turin, but takes more interest in the lectures on literature given by the poet Arturo Graf (1848-1913). Gozzano's law studies are never completed satisfactorily, and he never becomes a lawyer.

1906

At the Cultural Society in Turin he first makes the acquaintance of Amalia Guglielminetti (1885-1941) who is already famous as a poet.

1907

Publishes his first volume of poetry, *The way of refuge*, which contains early versions of "The two roads" and "The friend of Grandmother Speranza". The book is reviewed very favourably.

There is a worsening of the chest trouble from which he has suffered for some time, and he now starts to travel for his health.

Starts a long correspondence, a short love-affair, and a long friendship with Amalia Guglielminetti.

1911

Publishes *The colloquies*.

1912

Travels to India and Ceylon, where he certainly visits Bombay and Colombo but probably not most of the places described so vividly in his "letters from India" published in *La Stampa* and republished posthumously as a book in 1917 with the title *Towards the cradle of the world*.

1915

Italy enters the first World War.

1916

Gozzano dies, after receiving the sacraments, and is buried at Agliè.

THE COLLOQUIES

I
The youthful error

1. *The colloquies*

...to him, the veteran of Love and Death,
they lied to him, those two fine things, they lied...

I

I'm twenty-five now! Yesterday I wasn't.
Now I am old. My youth, now it has gone,
leaves me the present of not being present!

This book's about the past, but I restrain
the sob-stuff, and recall some raggedy
remains of my lost youth in every line.

I'm twenty-five! Think of the prodigy
by Joshua...and then watch my sun set
slowly but surely on a leaden sky.

I'm twenty-five... The thirties are in sight,
disturbing and disturbed by powerful urges
dying away...and then will come the fright-

ful forties, the most taciturn of ages,
and then old age itself, yes old age plied
with dentures and dyed hair and even crutches.

Now, oh my youth, never enough enjoyed,
I see you as you were, I recognise
your smile, my love not ever understood

but in the gloomy instant of goodbyes!
I'm twenty-five!... Now onward as I hobble
towards the final goal, I realise

that you were fine indeed, like some fine novel!

But a fine novel which in fact I never
lived through myself, but saw lived by that man
who used to follow me, my silent brother.

I wept and laughed for that brother of mine
who wept and laughed himself, and was so like
the ideal ghost of me, youthful and fine.

I turned around at every step, looked back,
curious over him, and fixed him keenly,
eavesdropping on his thoughts, now bright now black.

He thought the things which I repeated only,
living that life for me which I could not,
and comforting my grief when it was lonely.

He loves and lives this life which he finds sweet;
I merely told, in my artistic dream,
the tale when in the end it was complete.

I did not live, but dumbly upon dumb
paper portrayed him. Now I do not live.
Only, frozen and set apart, in him

I have to smile to see myself alive.

2. *The ultimate infidelity*

Sadness, sweet thing, you used to be the friend,
not long since, of the boy just back from school
having a bite to eat, bent over dull
Greek sentences that never seemed to end...

And later, what a sentimental stroll!
You and your adolescent, almost blind
with wild desire at the imagined sound
of one voice or one feminine footfall.

Sadness is fading fast away today
for ever from this weather-beaten heart,
where nothing but a grin against the grain

persists and twists my wretched mouth this way
and that... Oh, honestly I don't know what
's more sad than never to be sad again.

3. *The two roads*

Between the yellow and green of the broom upon each side
the shining alpine road followed the valley down.

Slow tedium now farewell! At an astonishing rate
a cyclist came in sight at the very top of the hill.

She reached us, alighted, and said: "Signora, I'm Grazia!"
She smiled with the grace and flair of her costume, a vivid plaid.

"You're Grazia? The little baby?" – "You recognise me still?"
And the older, with a will, embraced the younger lady.

"You are Graziella then! You're eighteen? How time flies!
How is your mother these days? How beautiful you've grown!

Graziella, after all! You were greedy and not very good!..."
"That time then, Signora, has stayed in your mind?" – "So beautiful,

yet you cycle all alone?" – "Yes." – "Will you come with us
on foot a little space?" – "Signora, the pleasure's mine..."

"May I present, meanwhile, this gentleman: a dear
friend of my husband, a lawyer. Give him your bicycle..."

She smiled and said no more. Along and up the hill
I wheeled that bicycle massed roses set on fire.

The lady, wiser and older, and the audacious child
went walking side by side, their arms about each other.

II

The one was truly young, and her skirt was rather short,
yet already a woman: pert, beautiful, dark, and strong,

26

with her collar standing up, a cravat knotted around,
and long loose hair unbound under a jockey cap.

And I savoured, without a word, sharp as the sharp aroma
that came from the firs, the aroma of her complete girlhood.

– O way of our salvation, with flowers on every side
like joys unharvested, O virgin apparition,

for me in my interim the right way of redemption
perhaps, or soothing potion to charm away the gloom!

O child, those hands of yours enclose my destiny;
to make my fated way down to Death by peaceful shores,

to go to Nothing, down, down by my human road,
but to hold you by the hand, O sweetly-smiling one!

So I spoke, without a word. And the other one, meanwhile,
I regarded: pitiful by the side of such girlhood!

Long beautiful that lady; soon beautiful no more
that lady who once saw Graziella as a baby.

Her eyes have that strange sorrowful beauty in them still
of a flower whose petals fall and shall have no tomorrow.

Under the sky, to me, beside that healthy girl,
how harsh, how terrible the havoc seemed to be!

Nothing more woebegone than that mouth was, brilliant red –
too red, than eyebrows dyed, than eyeshadow put on

round eyes that had grown dull, than lips in a sort of pleat,
than rouge and its deceit on a face that was too pale,

than, blazing blondily, hair as if set on fire,
much more serenely fair in times that used to be.

Long beautiful that lady; soon beautiful no more
that lady who once saw Graziella as a baby!

– O heart, what was the use of a morning that lit up
upon life's rugged slope roads that were only false?

Heart that was never in bloom, whom something vainly urges
to what are pure mirages in gardens not so glum,

you hardly think it clever for a man to stop and stare
or project through the dreaming air another *vita nuova*.

You'll go down to Nothing, down, down by your human road,
not holding by the hand the sweetly-smiling one;

and the other potion is yours, as long as life may linger:
Time is nothing if not stronger than all your courage is.

Such were my thoughts, I fear, as along and up the hill
I wheeled that bicycle massed roses set on fire.

III

Thick groves of firtrees grew right up the rugged slope
of the ravine right up to the barren ice and snow.

The scattered sluggish flocks were bleating and lowing, intent
on browsing rich milk from the mint while hanging from the rocks;

and the drowsy rhythm of bells ringing near and far around
combined with the rhythmic sound of torrents and waterfalls.

Begone for once dull care! The sharp scent of the firs
reaches the heart. Who cares if love does not appear?

An abundant scent, so fine who in the world can say
whether of resin? or of thyme? or of serenity?...

We paused by a meadow awhile, and the Signora inclined her
head, kissed the Signorina, and smiled in her farewell.

"Remember I'll wait for you, they'll all be waiting with me;
we'll have a cup of tea, and gossip a little bit too..."

"I'll come, Signora, I shall." In a rush from my hands she took
her bicycle right back. She did not thank me at all.

She did not speak. She got onto her bike with one bound,
and went with the rustling sound that is made by a naked foot,

by a flutter of wings unknown, as though accompanied
by something winged at the side as the wheels began to turn.

We paused to watch her go. The road, like a very thin
alabaster strip, curved down into the valley below.

"Signora!... Goodbye!..." Her shout blew back from a long way off.
Her teeth, from a long way off, flashed with a pearly light.

In the verdure she disappeared, and then appeared again.
"Signora!" we heard again. And that was the last we heard.

Grazia has gone. Yes, she has flown – where? – on her bicycle...
"And she didn't speak at all, no not a word to me!"

"That bothers you?" – "Well, yes!" – "She was silent, my love,
       for you,
as Suffering is silent too..." – "Or even Happiness..."

4.   *Eulogy of ancillary amours*

I

I seize upon that nimble servant who
is always full of gossip, on the go
as intermediary between us two.

I'm stirred by her fresh laughter, by the slow
waiting in vain, her sharp remarks, the hour,
the scent of something from Boccaccio...

She likes to mock, to struggle, to implore,
she even brings her mistress into play:
"How shameful it would be for her! My poor,

poor mistress!..." And she gives herself to me.

II

Like figures out of the *Decameron*,
maidservants give us, and without torment,
more healthy pleasure than the mistress can.

Not the shrewd pain the lady hard as flint
inflicts, not slow and sickly martyrdom,
and not the sort of tedious sentiment

which makes night long ("Oh, will sleep never come?"),
not, above all, the soul made sad by pleasure:
a calmer, much more masculine good time.

I praise the love of maidservants for ever!

5.   *The game of silence*

And did things really happen thus that day? Do
I actually recall that day in spring?
I do recall – or dream? – a velvet meadow,
I do recall – or dream? – skies blackening,
the lightning flashes and your panicking,
the livid squall, strange countryside in shadow...

And then the rustic dairy on the hill,
shouting, running, the housewife at the door,
the shelter for the night, the crazy while,
and you as happy as a milliner,
and dawn, and singing on the threshing-floor,
and then returning in a flowery veil...

– Talk to me! – But you went upon your way
climbing through blossoms of the peachtree, wet
with dew, white blossoms of the almondtree...
Stiff and unspeaking, and obsessed with what
is swiftly snatched, you brooded on about
what happens, no one ever knows just why...

– Talk to me! – I was following the trace
of scent left by your skirt... I see again
your slender shape of an effeminate man,
your knitted brows, your still unspeaking face;
it seems a dream of the finale when
it seems displeasing you that you should please...

And still you would not let me hear your voice.
I leaned towards you, pleading on the train
above the rapid rhythmic thunderous noise...
I shook you, giving you a dressing down,
I hurt you, and I all but struck you down,
and still you would not let me hear your voice.

Time flies, my happy friend, and takes away
all of life's promises and every hope.
To kisses and kind words it puts a stop...
But not that silence. In my memory
remains the mouth with not a word to say,
the mouth that in its silence said: Shut up!...

6. *The good companion*

It was not Love, no. But our senses were
becoming curious... And our cultivation
of dream was such... We thought the rapid action
certain to gather mystery more and more.

But after your last kiss, in which I wore
out my last kiss, after my last pulsation,
I only heard dry sobbing agitation
muffled in your abundant head of hair.

Hopeless to try to melt and fuse in one
two hearts dreaming and thought had petrified;
Love cannot hold equalities together.

No sentiment. We must become immune,
and stride more strongly out along the road,
allies and good companions, and for ever.

7. *Wintry*

Cre-eak! Cra-ack! A sudden noisy flaw
went arabesquing wildly through the ice.
"Get off! Get off!" we heard, not once but twice,
and everyone was making for the shore.
It was – encouraged by the blast of fear –
the fastest I have seen a crowd disperse.

"Stay on!" Our arms being linked, we stayed together,
and she made sure our fingers were entwined.
"Now, if you love me, you will stand your ground."
And so, on the deserted tricky mirror,
we stayed alone, spreading our wings together,
drunk with sheer space, deaf to the shouts around.

Now insubstantial almost as a ghost,
yielding myself in concert, there I was
cutting figures of eight upon the glass,
without a memory, without a past.
But ice was creaking at the edge more fast;
more sombre was the cracking of the ice.

I shuddered then like him who hears a laugh
and seems to recognise Death's croaking sneer,
and bending down, my eyeballs great with fear,
I saw our ashen faces, out of breath,
loom upwards from their sepulchre beneath.
Creak! Crack! at the ice's edge sounded more clear.

Oh now how I bewailed, my hand still tied,
bewailed the world and my sweet life within it!
The voice of instinct cannot be denied!
There is in life a pleasure, and I own it!
I pried my fingers loose and, having done it,
managed to reach, though short of breath, the side.

Now she alone, deaf to her shouted name,
went spinning round the kingdom where she reigned.
Till it pleased Her Highness finally to stand
once more on terra firma, eyes aflame,
her hair loose, throbbing, beautiful, like some
wing-folding stormy petrel on dry land.

What though she showed some breathlessness? She took
no notice but came sailing smoothly forward;
she did not see the ladies when they glowered;
she did not hear a sobersides' rebuke;
but smiled on me, said, "Thank you, sir", and shook
my hand a moment and hissed out, "You coward!"

8. *Absence*

A kiss. She's gone. She disappears
into the depths, where the wooded way
is lost to sight, that now appears
a corridor in the greenery.

I go back up where just before
she wore her beautiful grey dress:
I see the crochet-hook once more,
the novels, and every tiny trace...

I lean upon the balcony.
And on its rail I rest my cheek.
I am not sad. How could I be?
This very evening she'll be back.

Summer around is beginning to die.
Above a scarlet geranium hovers
a big swallow-tail butterfly,
vibrates its caudate wings and quivers...

Already on the wide serene,
where azure day seems infinite
and like a sheet of silk stretched tight,
the moon considers her return.

The frog is dumb. The pond is shining.
But suddenly a flash, a flare,
a great smaragdine blaze, a burning
ember of blue: the kingfisher...

I am not sad. I am, however,
when I look at the garden, bowled
over. By what? Who knows? I never
felt quite so much just like a child.

By what? Just by the things around.
The flowers look most peculiar.
And yet there are always roses, and
always geraniums blooming there...

9. *Banquet*

Sunset, and something that I do enjoy,
over the firedogs and the wheezing embers,
is calling up those few this heart remembers,
ladies who smiled at me along the way.

II

Enspirited already, they rise up,
all bodiless... Those who were distant, those
I thought of as companions full of hope,
some little, some most fleeting: actresses
maidservants courtesans and milliners
out of Boccaccio, witty keen and sharp...

Above the crackling logs they rise again,
among the sudden sparks, that ashen troop
of friends... Not Love, no! I have never known
true Love, for which so many laugh and weep:
Love has not touched me yet; now with no hope
I look about me for the ball and chain.

Unloved ones who once loved me, for Love's wound
in vain I offered up this empty heart.
Love never struck me with that cruel dart
which others found so sweet, or so it seemed...
What is this ice to which I am condemned?
Is there no help in herbs or magic art?

III

– From your nativity you've been accursed;
no magic art can help you through your dream!
You will take with you to the very tomb
a frozen heart, an all-consuming thirst.
Sad youngster, you knew nothing in the least.
What can one know when Love has never come?

But one will come and kiss you on the lips,
and lean upon the heart that you keep barred;
perhaps she is already knocking hard
with bony knuckles on your door, perhaps
she touches you upon the shoulder, laps
you in her sightless hair, and you're ensnared...

Their eyes are sisterly; they fade away
all all at once. The heart starts to recover.

"Since Love has always lied to you, sad brother,
we hope the other fine thing does not lie!"

II
On the threshold

10. *On the threshold*

I

You who laugh even through tears, my heart, like a cheerful lad,
my heart, like a child who is glad to live in this world of ours,

even enclosed in your shell, you often seem to hear
someone knock knock on the wall... It seems that the doctors
    are here.

In a kind of *vers libre*, knock knock, with their instruments and
    their machines
searching for some kind of signs, knock knock at the chest, front
    and back.

They discern some woodworm or rot, these old pundits... And
    to what end?
I would smile, except in the end I always have to pay out...

"Just here at the top of the lung...a tiny murmur...just here
on the shoulder-blade..." And they draw a ridiculous blue ring.

"Stop scribbling verses...eat better...and no more sleepless
    nights...
no women...no more cigarettes...and go where the skies are
    brighter:

Nervi...San Remo...Rapallo...to chase melancholy away;
and if you'll permit, my good fellow, we'll try radioscopy..."

The fearful heart – who knows? – may sense the penetration
of its dark close habitation by sudden chilly rays.

Into the thorax there flows a fluid which spreads around,
giving no pain or wound, to show on a background which glows

41

the bones, the organs, disease, like the lightning when it shows
a wood outlined, all the boughs in their tiniest intricacies.

They see some woodworm or rot, these old pundits... And to
    what end?
I would smile, except in the end I am always obliged to pay out.

III

You who laugh even through tears, my heart, like a cheerful lad,
my heart, like a child who is glad to live in this world of ours,

my heart, I greatly fear – it's only for you I'm unhappy –
the coming of the Lady called Death by all of us here.

(By men: for water and rock and grass and insect and poet
give her a name which, I know it, means something not gloomy
    or dark.)

She's a Lady dressed in a dress made of nothing; she has no form.
What she touches (she touches us) she always contrives to
    transform.

A sense of wellbeing will come like a nightmare with no hurt;
you will wake changed from without, in your face your hair your
    name.

From harmless nightmares you rise; you feel different, and distant,
    and *you* know
no more of the colloquies you held with guidogozzano.

Though I am left in pain, my heart in my breast, be dumb!
Like a bridegroom I'm serene and like a novice calm.

11. *Survival of the fittest*

Now this almighty youngster, square-shouldered, broad of chest,
with clear untroubled eyes makes mock of my decline;
dull thought, vain study, and caution he holds in deep disdain;
hard exercise he likes: it makes him more robust.

He is the branch you foster on the selfsame trunk, against
the barren empty branch, Death, when you intervene...
Oh, may he pluck life's roses, nor lack for any gain,
for women or for pleasure! Nature, it is but just.

And may he turn out lucky as I could never be!
This hope alone perhaps will soften my distress
at facing up to Nothing... On the edge of Time and Space
we still find comfort in still living in somebody.

I sink to your dark realms, Death, uncomplainingly;
I give you thanks, O Life, for what you have given thus
Far. I smile upon my brother... And then, resigned, I pass
the cup across to him. Already I feel I'm he.

12.   *Salvation*

A life that lasts five hours?
A life five ages long?...
I'll thank God for the stupor
that sends me slumbering...

I like the animation
of my small flighty soul;
but best would be sound slumber
before the evening fall.

The morning's lively laughter
can never come again.
The splendour of the daytime
dies before afternoon.

13.   *Paul and Virginia*

The children of misfortune

Have mercy, lovers! Hear
my prayer! Mercy on this ironical
desert of mine where such chimeras are!

I

I, once upon a time, was Paul. The name
Virginia stirs me still, and I am moved
to read again this book whose taste is sour;
now bent above it far in space and time
I must relive the years already lived,
and weep, a boy just back from school once more…
The dream I dream is clear:
the isle where I was born, where love was taught us;
again I see horizons I remember
legendary as the landscapes I remember,
where foreign mariners, in tranquil waters,
trade for exotic spices and rare timber…
And at the forest edge, with smiling eyes,
Virginia hesitant…
Clear from the misty past I see arise
the land of lost content,
the land I never knew, and recognise…

II

Sweet-smelling countryside! O lofty palms
drawn up erect against the open sky,
fans of green feathers rustling in the breeze!
Trunks oozing manna or elastic gums,
strong sandalwood, and gloomy ebony,
writhing lianas, ferns as big as trees!
Virginia, with all these
do you recall how spring would last for ever?
Recall the fields of indigo and tea,
the Viceroy, the Old Man, the Missionary?
Recall those academic tropics, rather

45

contrived, but in the style that pleases me?...
Recall a tinge, a tint
of eighteenth-century exotic? A scent
of peace? A potion from a fruit unknown
to me but clearly meant
to give a foretaste of oblivion?

III

We were brother and sister on each other's
lips. In its blessèd ignorance our youth
was helped by everything around all ways:
the simple way of life of our forefathers,
the turning back to the primeval truth
that Jean-Jacques dreamed of all his rebel days.
Of Arts, of Sciences –
ignorant of Research which fags us out,
of History, that disingenuous tale –
we lived an idyll on our distant isle;
of any other place we had no thought,
of any other time we had no feel.
Our mothers, each day's end,
taught us of Goodness, and they taught us Love,
the one true Credo; and
our prayers rose lazily at each day's end
to Our Father who art in heaven above...

IV

Seated together in the evening calm,
we'd mark the fireflies in perpetual motion
amongst the verdure of the Hermitage;
through spaces in the colonnaded palm-
trees we saw Luna sparkling on the ocean;
a wild chant reached us from the forest edge...
And with us sat the Sage
with many a polished, pointed illustration
(Homer or Virgil) to advise us well...
Through him we named the places on our isle

46

according to the rhetoric in fashion:
the Stream of Amity, and Lily Hill,
the Fountain of Pure Speech...
That was the time when moral Nestors flourished,
sages skilful to preach,
the time of *sentiment* when ideals such
as *virtue* and *simplicity* were nourished.

V

Free from the competition always blazing
out in the sad world, we grew up contented
with what the net and dart provide; we two
handsome and happy as an old engraving
to illustrate your narrative; we sprinted
across the lakes in our swift bark canoe;
as woodland people do
we reckoned up the hour, the day, the year:
"How old would you be then?" "Beside the door
you see those disparate palms? As old as those..."
"When will you come?" "When mangoes are in flower..."
"Sister, the leaves are starting now to close,
the first of the stars to glister..."
"This tall tree's shade is shrunken to the root:
it is midday, my sister..."
Such was the life we led, the very best, a
life for the Fauns, for Dryads, for delight.

VI

Then came that time which leaves me out of heart.
An aunt, anxious to add you to her vast
French acres, had her will, though you were loth.
The Viceroy had you hustled to the port
by barbarous servants! So in tears you passed
for ever from this blessèd plot, this earth,
this most of all things worth
your love, to tempt the wandering waves of ocean!
I lived, scarce conscious of my evil star,

47

with the grieved mothers and the sable nation;
I called you, and in stones and vegetation
I saw your figure all in white, a clear
impossibility...
One hopeless year concluded... Then there came
Father Baptiste one day
to tell us of your flight and your return,
the Saint-Géran in sight beyond the bay!

VII

With the two mothers, and half-crazed with joy,
I ran down to the shore: "My bride has come!
Virginia has come back to be my bride!..."
But now the Storm is rising on the sea,
a very beautiful and stylised storm
as shown in ancient paintings of the Flood.
A sail! A sail! We dread
to see the ship again in quick cross lightning,
where mournful stormy petrels make their moan,
white albatrosses. Waves and sky are one
apocalyptic horror. It is frightening
to watch the Saint-Géran as it is thrown
about the Indian Ocean.
We hear the waters howl and boil and bubble,
and then a human shriek through the commotion,
terrible in its trouble:
"Virginia must be saved from this destruction!..."

VIII

The Saint-Géran is sinking. Her tough crew
attempt to save her, but she is a wreck.
When all is lost, they leap into the water.
She's breaking on hard coral. The first few
tremendous waves are trembling on the deck.
The wind so strong. Sails, masts, and rudder shatter...
Virginia stands apart, a
pale solitary shape!... A naked sailor

tries to remove her dress to plunge with him
into the sea; but such Virginia's shame
(the rhetoric in vogue!) she spurns her saviour
and makes her hands a shield... The rest is doom.
One gloomy ripple; and it is the last;
it quickly dies away...
No vessel sighted in the lightning flash...
My sobs are silenced by
the sobbing of the ocean, all too vast.

IX

Then the day dawned. There was your lovely body
cast down among contorted hydrozoa,
seeming to sleep and sleep most peacefully,
Silent I bend above that face to study
how the pale violet of death stood there
still mingled with the rose of modesty...
Grief without remedy!
Grief without weeping, hopeless grief without
a clamour! Dead you lay, your dream unbroken;
you came back dead to one who could but wait!
Your right hand held my portrait, our love-token,
your left was pressed against a broken heart...
"Virginia! O my dreams!
Virginia!" So I called. "Virginia!"
My eyes were glazed. "You are the Love which comes
back Death! Love... Death..." And then I spoke no more.

X

I died for love. I am reborn. I live
once more, but not to love. The dream is gone
for ever, and the heart will bloom no more.
I call on Love. Love is so fugitive.
My Muse is all in mourning but in vain;
she weeps and mourns for everything of yore.
You'll find my dead heart there
with you, in all the island's tropic growth,

49

where palms are groaning low and scarcely moving,
lined out along the Bay of Burning Faith...
Oh, were I but, as I am loved, but loving,
I'd sing in such a novel way my troth!
But this corroded soul,
caught in the evening chill, can only sneer...
Have mercy, lovers! Hear
my prayer! Mercy on this ironical
desert of mine where such chimeras are!

14. *La signorina Felicita* or *Felicity*

10 July: Saint Felicity

I

Signorina Felicita, this hour
finds evening falling on your ancient home
and ancient garden. And the memories come
upon me thick and fast. I see once more
you and Ivrea and the skyblue Dora,
all that dear region which I do not name.

It's Saint Felicity's Day! And I am bound
to wonder at this hour what you are doing.
Roasting coffee? The aroma's all around.
Thinking of me while you are singing, sewing?
Thinking of how the lawyer's not returned?
And here's the lawyer wondering what you're doing.

He's thinking of the autumn days long gone,
Vill'Amarena crowning the long rise,
the Marchesa in her ruin, cherrytrees,
the kitchen-garden with the box's mourn-
ful scent, and all the broken glass upon
the circling wall, which has seen better days...

Vill'Amarena! Oh what gentle charm
invests you this September, and what peace!
Up to its highest gable all the house
is clothed about with shocks of maize: like some
great lady (late baroque) discourteous Time
devours, who put herself in peasant dress.

Sad uninhabited fine edifice!
Big-bellied gratings rust away and writhe!
Silence and stealth of rooms! Nothing alive!
An odour of the past pervades the house!
An odour of abandoned emptiness!
Legends are fading on the architrave!

51

The centaur Nessus, Hercules' loud roar,
heroic deeds of Homer's great explorer,
the sungod's son, the north Italian river,
Ariadne, Minos, and the Minotaur,
the flying Daphne as the god draws near
transmuted into laurel, green for ever...

Think of the furnishings – how very sad! –
think of the furnishings, severe and dull,
ancient and new: the pokerwork gone mad
on Grecian sofas in the Empire style,
and tucked inside a looking-glass la Belle
Otero on a postcard... Very sad!

Elegant ancient household on the wane!
Enormous cupboards absolutely full
of sheets you mend with patience... Handed-down
simplicity to comfort and console,
simplicity that's immemorial!
The simple life, your father, you, alone!

II

And that good rustic father – said to be
a usurer – made me at home without
being worried that I was so much about,
and talked of grapes, and deferentially
confided how an old catastrophe
at law had left him in a sorry state.

"You, as a lawyer..." and he'd fuss and fidget,
and draw me to the drawing-room, and read
out something very slowly and in secret.
Docile, I'd listen to the dusty deed,
distracted by the smell of ink gone bad,
distracted by the pattern in the carpet,

distracted by that room, too big and dark...
"...and the Marchesa fled... The wild expenses..."
distracted by the hangings' Grecian edges...

"...of eighteen-ten, and yet the records mark..."
distracted by the rheumy clock's tic-toc...
"...the mortgagee being dead, the mortgage hence is..."

At last he sees my understanding fails
and he's dismayed: "The mortgagee is dead,
dead, dead!" – "And if, you see, as I have said,
he's dead, well then..." Well then, as fortune wills,
you stand at last in front of us, all smiles:
"Here's our imaginary invalid!"

III

You're almost ugly, no attractiveness
comes from your clothing, it's so countrified,
and yet your honestly domestic face,
your bright hair, coloured like the sun and tied
and twisted up in many a tiny braid,
make you the type of Flemish loveliness...

And now I see your scarlet mouth once more,
laughing and drinking how it widens mightily,
see your square countenance, no eyebrows there,
all over it is freckled very lightly,
and see your steady eyes shining so brightly,
sky-blue as cups and saucers often are...

You loved me. With your smiling steady eyes
you flattered, with your feminine demeanour
you flirted. In so many obvious ways
you only wished to please me, Signorina:
I have known city conquests, but no finer
allurement than your simple wish to please!

Each day I used to climb in your direction,
which took me on a steep and sunlit way.
The chemist had no notion, I must say,
that there would grow between us such affection,
when he presented on that first occasion
the unknown stranger there on holiday.

Sometimes – the table being already set –
you invited me to supper. I enjoyed
the oldtime meal, such simple plates we had
with florid patterns, and the moth, the cat,
decrepit Maddalena, talk of food,
siestas, and a game of cards and that...

Towards nine or so there would assemble there,
for cards, the entire illustrious faculty
of local statesmen, viz. the Notary
Public, the Doctor, and the honoured Mayor;
but – since I was an absentminded player –
those gentlemen did not think much of me...

I found things were much pleasanter and cleaner
among the brightly-coloured crockery:
our silence in that kitchen, Signorina,
the garlic and the basil, could not be
but very very comforting to me,
mixed with the lemon scent of the verbena...

Maddalena with a steady muffled mutter
stacked up the dishes, grumbling all the time,
washing up slowly, and I stood beside her,
adrift in a completely different dream,
tuning my verse's syllables in time
to the steady rhythm of the dishes' clatter.

Under the massive chimney cowl (in me
the soul of some dead cook is alive once more
perhaps) I loved the hissing of the fire;
the song of a singing cricket seemed to say
word upon word to my attentive ear,
I saw Pinocchio and my destiny...

I saw what bit of life is still to come:
I closed my eyes against a future full
of worry; I reopened them: your smile
brought hope again to flourish in full bloom!

Upon our ears what bursts of laughter fell,
what witty sayings, from that other room.

IV

The restful splendour of an attic-room
wherein a hundred years of refuse sleeps!
Within that tomb, among the wasted shapes
of what was once and never will return,
the Lady loomed in the enormous frame
so white so beautiful she stopped my steps:

"Her luck being out, she handed the house down
to my grandfather's grandfather... We close
her up inside this attic-room because
she brings bad luck... She has at times been seen
to leave the picture; under the new moon
her step is heard along the corridors..."

Echoes prolong each footstep as it goes
among such odds and ends of time gone by,
and the Marchesa with the Grecian nose,
high-waisted, seen beneath a pagan sky
one bare foot in her hand, takes her repose
umbrageous in a grot of Arcady.

About her, smiling in her Grecian dress
and Grecian dream, who came to die of hunger,
there lay a tattered and promiscuous race:
some furniture, some oil lamps, the odd hamper,
mattresses, rats' nests, crockery: the lumber
that since it is rejected charms my Muse!

We poked among the rubbish to uncover
some old engravings of illustrious people,
and found a head adorned with noble laurel
was *Tasso in the gardens at Ferrara*.
"You are a lawyer. Tell me, why'd they bother
with sprigs of cherry on these funny people?"

55

I could not help but laugh to hear you say so.
We paused awhile. It all seemed so absurd.
What's glory in an attic-room alas? Oh,
three hampers, and an Empire-style commode,
a sable frame around an ugly head,
and then the name beneath: Torquato Tasso!

Just then, among that load of learned lumber,
my eyes were drawn to the autumnal plain,
baroque and oval-shaped, as it had been –
the crowded little panes of the old dormer
distorted so the enamelled panorama –
an unrealistic painting of the scene.

Untrue (and beautiful) enamelled squares,
or so the Canavese now appeared:
the Serra's even line, churches, and trees,
the hills about Montalto, turreted
Ivrea; and my dream of peace was spread
beyond that high and shining place of peace.

Here's the Vill'Amarena then – I thought –
there the Delectable Mountains, and beyond
what martyrs call the World: that thing all fraught
with strife and stormy commerce without end,
where hordes of "two-legged thingummies" abound
provoking us to pity for their lot...

The Leveller has their graves already made,
but they go on, exchanging knock for knock,
distinguished, broken down into this bloc
and that, as diverse fancies take the lead:
exactly like a swarm of ants all red,
exactly like a swarm of ants all black...

In sunlight or the shadow of the Cross,
how money whirls them like a hurricane;
till who can hear, O Muse, the quiet tone
and gentle rhythm of a still small voice?
Better withdraw at once from all these wars
for pleasure, money, or the laurel-crown...

56

The laurel-crown... Oh, what a baby, what
an innocent I was! The laurel-crown
these days is kept for him who blossoms out
on hearing trumpets blown (he blows his own),
who hogs the limelight, who's a charlatan
never quite happy till he's talked about...

"But you're not talking now. What's wrong? Please say."
"Signorina, just think of what I do
down in the city and its misery...
It would be pleasant to stay here, with you!"
"Here, in the attic?..." "For eternity!"
"For ever? You want that?" "I really do!"

And then I stopped. I happened to remark
a death's-head moth. It graced the wall, alone,
a peaceful prisoner, the fearful sign
occluded since its wings were folded back.
When I began to tickle it, it woke,
to hover with a low lamenting whine.

"What a sad buzz!" "The Marchesa in her pain...
It must be her ruined soul bringing bad luck..."
What could we hear? Our moth upon the rack,
and singing from the vineyards now and then:
Oh, how I'm struck with you, my handsome man,
and by a siren's song the sea is struck...

Then from below a mournful, muffled call:
"That's Maddalena, pained because we're late;
we must go down; it's time for supper!" "Wait!
Look at the sunset... Like a fiery ball!...
Let's wait a while!" "We'll have to go, it's late!"
"Oh, Signorina, let us wait a while!..."

Our foreheads to the glass, above the plain,
we marked the black bats, an enormous crowd;
bells rang to reach us on the wind, the sun
was lost to sight among the broken cloud;
across the Canavese countryside
night slowly more and more made itself known...

"Look, there's a star!..." "Three stars!..." "There are four stars!..."
"Five stars!" "Does it not seem to you that we
are dreaming?" But you rose, rebellious
against crepuscular uncertainty:
"We must go down! It's late: who knows, they may
incline to think the very worst of us..."

V

What blessed spells of idleness, at noon
in the ancestral park where some slight trace
still lingered of the epoch that had gone!
The Seasons – armless, broken-nosed, of course,
knee-deep in dung and grapeskins – nonetheless
looked over leeks and lettuce in disdain.

The leeks and lettuce (useful things) were growing
by box-hedge and by flowers as if in scorn,
where cabbage-whites were fluttering in the sun,
chafers, and bumblebees whose days are flying...
I went on whispering, and you went on sewing
intoxicated by the sound I spun.

"How altered are my likes and my dislikes!
Could I stay by your side till kingdom come,
and here, what with white linen and green leeks,
finish that bit of life that's still to come!
Oh, if you only knew how tired I am
of all those ladies modelled upon books!

A lady came, her heart upon her sleeve;
then many others: all have gone away.
From you alone this cold dreamer might have
some training for the tender prodigy:
never ever upon my leaden sky
arose the dawn of what they christen: Love..."

You stared at me... In your bright eyes I read
a sort of vague indefinite alarm;
I sought your hands and held them both in mine

58

awhile above the needlework, and said:
"Dear Signorina, only tell me, would
you marry me if I were well again?"

"Why do you make me speeches such as those?
Marry? You…me…ugly, without a bean?…"
And low on that low bench you huddled down,
cupping your hands until they hid your face,
all with that shrill peculiar sobbing noise
which silly little schoolgirls feign in fun.

Looking closer, I came to realise
you were shaking like someone sobbing out
her heart, and not quite able to compose
herself: I seemed to catch your voice cut short
by some last strangled hiccups in your throat:
"Don't ever make…speeches again…like those!"

"You're weeping?" And I tried to raise your head
and tried in vain. So, with a straw, I took
to tickling your soft ear, your slender neck…
All smiles at once and shining far and wide
you raised yourself again recomforted,
and trilled out trills as from a finch's beak.

Woman: endlessly lovely, and opaque!

VI

You loved me. With your shining steady eyes
you flattered, with your feminine demeanour
you flirted. In so many obvious ways
you only wished to please me, Signorina:
I have known city conquests, but no finer
allurement than your simple wish to please!

To merge my life for ever with your life
here in the hundred-year-old house! Yes here –
with you making for me a lively wife,

with you transparent as the very air
we breathe – recant the faith in literature
which gives us such a very deathly life...

A sterile life, the life of reverie!
It is a better life, rugged and real,
the tradesman leads, intent on a good deal,
goaded indeed by sharp necessity
but still alive! I feel the infamy
of being a poet in this age at all!

You're not. You are a cutter-out and stitcher
of father's shirts. You've been to junior school
where they told you, though you were sceptical,
the world was round... You never think of Nietzsche...
I could be happier with such a creature
than with some whining intellectual...

Those ills we have, how could you comprehend?
I like you for your unassuming ways,
your great contentment in the daily round,
which does not stretch to understanding these
verses of mine for you. You really please
me more the more you fail to understand.

And I don't wish to go on being me!
Not the cold aesthete, nor the sophist, rather
one living in your home town happily,
one living for the little he can gather
by steady trading in obscurity,
just like the chemist, and just like your father...

And I don't wish to go on being me!

VII

The chemist lauded in his pharmacy
a medicine that was miraculous:
"This super soporific will bring peace

60

all night and every night, rely on me!"
He showed, meanwhile, a certain jealousy,
and showed it with a savage wordiness.

"He's mad about her, really on the hook!
That notary! A funny fellow that!
The Signorina's plain, her chest is flat,
and she is very vulgar, like a cook...
Her dowry is minute, for heaven's sake:
ten thousand, or perhaps not even that..."

"And so?" "The notary is wild with you,
with me who introduced you (a mistake!);
he doesn't say hello, he doesn't speak..."
"He's jealous?" "Jealous? He's consumed with woe!..."
"Mere gossip!..." "Well, I won't disguise from you
that I much fear me there'll be ugly talk..."

"Fear not! I'm going." "Going? Far away?"
"Yes, very far... The talk will disappear,
you'll see, when there's no colour any more."
"And when d'you go?" "In a week I'm on my way..."
Ipecacuanha wafts me on my way
under a full moon in the cool night air.

September. Through the moonlight's friendly calm
sad as a tramp I wandered on my way.
Midnight was striking loud and long and high
through that dear region which I do not name.
I saw the moon above the bell-tower gleam
out "like a dot upon a massive i".

In many sad dreams, few you could call gay,
I wandered all around with my regret
alone by hedge, by vine, by chestnut-tree
all silvered over in the bright moonlight;
and lingered by the cemetery-gate
as people do in books of poetry.

You who already on the other side
are resting, freed from joy and from distress,
speak to the sated pilgrim! What's the use
of getting well?... Of living?... So, you dead,
you recommend the furtive Host instead
who frees us from the bounds of Time and Space?

And so awhile I mused, pressing my head
against the bars. Almost as if in scorn
screech-owls were screeching out their antiphon...
The Moon, imprisoned by the bars, displayed
with her bizarre effects of light and shade
two lovers always kissing on and on.

A lunar kiss, where clouds are brightening up,
such as was à la mode some seventy
years back! See Death here with Felicity!
This comes, that other always rushes up;
that exiles me across the vasty deep,
this promises some good that there may be...

VIII

That melancholy day of our farewell
merely to see your villa made me glad.
Summer was dying peacefully indeed
that cloudless morning as I climbed the hill
past vines already bare, past meadows full
of lilac saffron, brilliantly bad.

It must have been the floricidal sight
of that bright flower presaging autumn mist
which made the swallows set about their first
uncertain efforts for their certain flight;
to me it seemed a warning that I might
do worse than wander with them south by west.

"I'm off today, right on the swallows' tails..."
"Where to?" "It hardly seems to matter whither...
I take this journey to avoid another...
Perhaps beyond Morocco to strange isles
rich in bananas, dates, essential oils,
lost in the mad Atlantic's fuss and bother...

Signorina, if I should come again
would you be mine still? And could I be sure
of finding you once more? And would this pure
love bring us to a blessed union?"
I saw your mouth pronouncing in return
very slowly the syllables: *I swear.*

You swore to me and drew upon the wall
arrows entwined with violets, and wove in
initials, and the date beside it all:
September the thirtieth, nineteen-o-seven...
I didn't smile. Deep down inside I even
enjoy romantic gestures straight from school.

The swallows were enough to deafen one:
they twittered out a kind of farewell prattle;
they flashed about, swift as a weaver's shuttle,
the weathered migrants urging the new-born...
You followed on the pathway to the sun
each fleeing flock until it grew too little...

"Another flock is off!..." "See how they swarm!"
"They've gone..." "And yet you didn't say goodbye!..."
"To you, but not to them, I say goodbye:
their road and my road are the very same:
some few days and I'll see them all again
down in a grove of palms in Barbary..."

Then came the time for parting; truly bitter
that parting from another century:
ladies in crinolines, each hair in order,
leaned out of gardens that appeal to me
and, sobbing very loudly, waved goodbye
to diligences making for the border...

You seemed a lady weeping, in some frantic
lyric of Prati's, someone on his way
to undiscovered isles in the Atlantic;
I too was from another century,
a good old sentimental young romantic…

The man I never am, but feign to be!

15. *The friend of Grandmother Speranza*

28 June 1850

"...to Speranza
from her Carlotta..."
(the dedication of a photograph in an album)

I

The stuffed parrot and the bust of Alfieri, the bloom
stuck in Napoleon's frame (good things in the worst of taste),

the dismal fireplace, sweet-boxes with no sweets,
the made-of-marble fruits sheltered by domes of glass,

some rather rare odd bits, jewel-cases from seashells,
the *Greetings* and what else, the bunches of coconuts,

Venice made of mosaic, the faded aquatints,
the caskets, the various prints, albums, florid, archaic,

d'Azeglio's canvases, and all the miniatures,
daguerreotypes with figures dreaming perplexities,

the chandelier well placed to multiply and increase
a thousandfold in its glass good things in the worst of taste,

the cuckoo-clock, loud and lofty, the seats which damasks adorn
with crimson...and I am reborn, reborn in eighteen-fifty!

II

The little brothers, they say, must enter the room with care
(the covers are off every chair). Today is a holiday.

And yet they burst in in a band. Now she's arrived, how they
    missed her!
Speranza their elder sister, and with her Carlotta her friend!

Grandmother is seventeen! Carlotta is almost as old,
and recently they've been told they may wear the crinoline,

and its hoop has the skill to render the skirt a ripple of roses.
From the crinoline arises the waist of a wasp more slender.

They both have shawls with a blaze of bird and fruit and flower;
parted sedately, their hair descends each side of the face.

They're top of the class. What knowledge! How anxiously they
     worked,
and never ever shirked! Now they have finished with college.

Children, let's have some peace! The friends – now don't be
     naughty! –
will essay on the pianoforte some ancient melodies.

Artificial melodies, affected and grandiose,
tunes of Arcangelo's and of Alessandro Scarlatti's.

Lovers under a curse, who groan over *heart* and *eyes*,
Giordanello's dreamy sighs in pleasant ugly verse:

> ...my dearest dove,
> believe I love!
> Bereft of you
> I fade and die!
> Such faithfulness
> must ever sigh,
> unless you cease
> your cruelty!...

Speranza is on the keys. Carlotta is singing. The song
opens life out with its thronging thousand promises.

What wonders from music's soft hints! Now both in the depth of
     their soul
see their betrothèd smile: the famous Handsome Prince,

the husband longed for in dreams... Trusting to fate, they would
pull
the petals off daisies in school to Prati's tender rhymes!

III

The Uncle arrives, a good sir, a man who has some standing,
much tied to the past, and depending on the Austrian Emperor.

And the Aunt is similar, and very respectable,
much tied to the past, but full of love for the King of Sardinia.

"Kiss Uncle and Aunt on the hand," so say Mamma and Papa,
and raise their faces on fire to the restive little band.

"And this is Speranza's friend who's with us for the summer,
the clever Carlotta Capenna of whom Speranza's so fond."

"Well then...well then...well then..." says the Uncle, the man
of repute,
slow-thinking hypocrite, "well then...well then...well then...

I knew a Capenna, I did, an Arturo Capenna... Capenna...
Indeed! At the court of Vienna! Indeed...indeed...indeed..."

"Perhaps some muscatel?" "My sister would be delighted."
Soon, smiling sedately, they're seated and the talk begins to swell.

"La Brambilla was really not such..." "For *Ernani* he's far too
stout..."
"No more sopranos about..." "That Verdi, oh what a touch!"

"In March there's to be a new piece at the Phoenix, or so I've been
told.
Rigoletto I think it's called. There's talk of a masterpiece."

"Is blue being worn, or grey?" "And these earrings! But those
rubies! These cameos!" "In Paris the novelty..."

"Radetzky? The ceasefire, and thence...well, peace, peace is the
      winner..."
"That youthful King of Sardinia is a man with plenty of sense!"

"He's tireless, it's true, and indeed he's most watchful and strong
      and shrewd..."
"Is he handsome?" "That couldn't be said." "He's certainly fond
      of the ladies..."

"Speranza!" (one bends to speak in a rather sibylline tone)
"Carlotta! Why not go down and play at shuttlecock!"

The happy friends then and there both curtsy very sedately
and take their leave most politely from the very respectable pair.

IV

A shuttlecock, as they play, is so forcibly returned
it fails to redescend from the height of a horse-chestnut tree!

They lean on the banisters and gaze on the lake, both filled
with thoughts of the love foretold in their dreams of seventeen
      years.

"If you saw his teeth, I say!" "How old is he?" "Twenty-eight."
"A poet?" "He's seen at the court of the famous Contessa Maffei!"

The day does not wish to fade. It kindles again and again
in a purple glow, like a dawn which is stigmatised in blood.

At last, though slowly, it's gone. The mountains go into mourning:
the Sun takes off his gold clothing, the Moon puts her silver on.

Moon, romantic, aureoled, who touch the very tops
of the poplars with your lips, moon curved like the brow of a child,

the dream of a past and more is encamped where you're gently bent:
are you not out of a print from *The Illustrated Stories*?

Have you seen the house, now deserted, of the beautiful Parisina?
Perhaps, perhaps you have been the one who was loved by Young
    Werther?

"Now! Dreams of what might be!" "The Lake has become very thick
with stars." "Now what do you think?" "I don't." "Would it please
    you to die?"

"Yes." "The sky seems to disclose more stars in the water and
    gleams.
Let us lean on the rail, let our dreams take place between two skies."

"I seem in suspense! I hover…" "He knows Mazzini even…"
"And you love him?" "His verse is heaven!" "That volume, he
    was the giver,

where so-and-so had to pine in luckless love, and where
he killed himself for her whose name was the same as mine!"

                                V

Carlotta! Your name is not fine, but a sweet thing like those scents
which call back the diligence, the shawl, the crinoline…

My grandmother's friend, I now make my way through walks
        where you read
of Jacopo's fate, so sad, in Foscolo's tender book.

I gaze at the album, your gift, the inscription and the date:
June the twenty-eighth, eighteen hundred and fifty.

You look like one rapt in a verse: to heaven your glance goes up,
your finger is on your lip – a rather romantic pose.

That day, which is no more, you had put on a rose-red dress
for the very latest craze – a *portrait photographer*…

Never seen in such youth again ever, Grandmother's friend, you
        are gone.
Yet you are the only one I could love perhaps, love as a lover!

16. *Cocotte*

Again I've seen our garden, and the one
next door, the palmtrees standing by the road,
and the rough railings from whose other side
she gave a sugared almond...

      "Little one,
what is that game you're playing, all alone?"
"I'm playing at the Universal Flood."

I showed my bucket, and the oddities
modelled in sand to adorn my little stage;
and she bent down as though she felt an urge
to kiss me with an impulse to reverse
the action, to withdraw; and through the bars
she kissed me like a bird inside a cage.

Her charming face will stay with me, I know,
seen from behind square bars, throughout my life!
She seized my head as though she were a thief;
I was amazed to find myself held so,
so closely held, her face and mouth close to,
so very different from my mother's mouth!

"You like the look of me then, little one?
You've come here for the bathing? That house there?"
"Yes... Here are Mummy and Daddy over here."
She let me go at once; her face took on
a dreamy look (I realised later on)
a dream of motherhood and of despair...

"She's a cocotte!..."

      "Mummy, what does that mean?"
"It means the lady is a wicked one:
you mustn't ever talk to her again!"

70

The clucking sound of that Parisian
title – co-co-tte – loaded my childish brain
with silly notions of an egg and hen...

I thought of all the fabled deities:
the sailors sailing for the Happy Isles...
Co-co-tte... Bad fairies with their evil spells
concealed in food and drink... Though no one says
what kind they are, I know their wicked ways,
the way they practise their mysterious skills!

III

One day – days later – she called out to me
behind the bars (verbena was in flower):
"You do not seem to like me any more!..."
"You're really a cocotte then, as they say?"
She kissed me, laughing rather desperately;
her eyes were full of melancholia.

IV

Among the disappointments, the dead joys,
twenty years on, your smile comes back today...
Where are you, wicked lady? Can you be
alive? How do you hide from prying eyes
(for you it were much better not to be!)
the terrible descent of all the years?

Now that the rouge is very little use,
the hair-dye, and the lipstick, and the powder,
your room stands empty of your final lover...
Except that one – the little elf or nis
you gave a sugared almond and a kiss –
twenty years on contrives to rediscover

you in his dream, and loves you in his dream,
and says: From my pure childhood, from that morning
perhaps I've loved but you alone, my darling!

Perhaps but you alone! I'm calling. Come!
If you should ever read these verses, come
back to the one who waits for you, my darling!

What matter now if you are not the same?
I am not four years old. I now desire
you dressed in time! It's now that I require
your past! I'll make you beautiful again –
Carlotta, Graziella are the same –
as all the ladies of my dreaming are.

My dream is nourished by the letting-go
and the regret. I love the roses that
I did not pick. What do I love but what
might well have come about but didn't?... So
I see the roses and the house and that
garden brought back from twenty years ago!

Your garden, still unchanged behind the bars,
among Ligurian eucalyptus still
stretches away... Come to the sated soul.
If I may see again that face the years
have ruined, I shall kiss that face of yours
until your mouth is once more beautiful.

If you should come, 'twould be as if you came
to bring me back myself as I was then.
The lady and the child will talk again.
We shall arise from the abyss of time.
If you should come, 'twould be as if I came
to bring you back yourself, young once again.

III
The veteran

17. Totò Merùmeni

I

With its untended garden, its spacious rooms, and its fine
seventeenth-century balconies alive with verdure,
the villa appears to be taken from certain verses of mine,
a model villa almost, out of a children's reader...

Sadly the villa dreams of better days, it dreams
of happy parties under hundred-year-old trees,
of lustrous banquets in enormous dining-rooms,
of dances in the hall despoiled by antiquaries.

But where in another age the Ansaldos used to come,
the Rattazzis, d'Azeglios, Oddones, now a motor-car
arrives and grinds to a kind of shuddering halt and some
shaggy stranger rattles the Gorgon on the door.

Somewhere a dog barks, and somewhere a step is heard,
the door half-opens... That silence, cloistral, barrack-like,
is where Totò lives with a mother who is sick,
a whitehaired great-aunt, and an uncle who is mad.

II

Totò is twenty-five, his temper is disdainful,
he is cultured, and he has a taste for inkhorn terms,
slight brain, and slighter scruple, and a rather painful
clearsightedness: in fact, the true child of our times.

Not rich, when the dreadful hour arrived for "selling ink"
(as Petrarch almost put it), a drunken journalist,
Totò chose exile. Now he's at liberty to think
of his errors, on which silence were no doubt best.

He is not bad. He sends cash to the needy man;
his friend gets choice fruit out of season in a basket;
the schoolboy runs to him, who wants his homework done;
the emigrant who needs a word is right to ask it.

75

So cold, so conscious of himself and every wrong,
he is not bad. He is the *good man* mocked by Nietzsche:
"...in truth I have to mock that ninny of a creature
who is called good because his talons are not strong."

Hard on his serious studies he goes down to play
with his best friends on the inviting garden plot.
And these best friends of his are: a loud-mouthed raucous jay,
an ape called Makakita, and a pussy-cat.

III

Life took back every promise she ever made to him.
He dreamed of actresses, princesses (it was torture),
he dreamed for years of a love that never ever came,
and now today the eighteen-year-old cook's his lover.

While all the house is asleep, that girl, her feet quite bare,
fresh as a ripened plum in the coldness of daybreak,
comes to his room, kisses his mouth, and then and there
leaps onto him in bed, flat on his blessèd back.

IV

Totò knows no emotion. A slow uncured distress
has dried up at their source the very founts of feeling;
of this man has been made, by dry analysis,
what flames make of a house through which the wind is howling.

But as a ruin fire has gutted may express
a swarm of irises, those marvellously bright things,
just so this withered soul puts forth, but less and less,
some few consolatory verses, rather slight things.

V

And so Totò Merùmeni, after sad days,
is almost happy. He alternates research and rhyme.
Shut in himself, he thinks, he grows, explores, and knows
the Life of the Spirit which he never knew one-time.

Because the voice is tiny, and so wide the scope
of the chosen art, and Time – while I am speaking – flies,
he works in isolation, smiles, and lives in hope.
He's living still. One day he's born. One day he dies.

18. *A woman reborn*

"I asked; but no one could say
how to find the distant home
of the hermit you have become.
I'm here. Am I in the way?"

"No!... But I am nonplussed.
It's vanity, I suppose,
but I do feel ill at ease
that I am so scruffily dressed.

You'll find your good companion
much changed: untidy, and even –
I must admit – unshaven,
with a corduroy jacket on!..."

"Oh Guido! Between us two!
Think what our past once meant.
Rough jacket or starched front,
you always will be you..."

With silent tenderness
she firmly pressed my hand,
like one who keeps in mind
some small chance of success.

And, sisterly, she gave
perhaps a glimpse of her –
gentle, familiar –
I might have been able to love.

II

"It's like a gentle doze,
enjoyable, not rowdy;
I read, I work, I study,
philosophise and laze...

78

My life today is sweet,
without a reason why;
from me has been taken away
who knows what heavy weight..."

"Desire, friend! Amorous rage!
Desire, now it is slain,
has left you with the calm
smile of an ancient sage...

And you are lucky! I,
in my dreaming and my unrest,
suffer from all of the vast
world I can't occupy!

I still dream of a dawn
unwitnessed by these eyes;
and oh desire still cries
dreadfully for that dawn!..."

She looked at the flowers, the books,
my unassuming room:
"And so this is your room!
Where is it that one works?"

"There! Very few things are held
in that lab of mine for sure..."
We passed through the décor
of that deceptive world.

A sort of rustling hiss
came from her skirt as she came
through the doorway with her mundane
and desecrating grace...

"These yellow salts you have
preserved in this dark glass?"
"Something mysterious:
crystals, and how they love."

"They love?..." – "From certain signs
that's how it now appears.
The wise break down barriers,
and unite the Three Domains.

The gulf of the unknown
is already opened up
under the microscope,
and the living, conscious stone...

The dogma of Matter seems used
up now. In everything
Essence is absolute king,
the Spirit is diffused..."

She paused to take it in,
with concentrated eyes
under her curving brows,
her hands under her chin,

so elegant, so slim
in her dress's rosy sheath,
her hair's black wavy wealth
enclosed in a towering helm.

"What's hung up in that urn
with the thick net around?"
"Chrysalids sleeping sound
and waiting for their turn..."

"How strange they are! How bright!
Gold pendants!... I would like
to pick them: they would make
a marvellous carcanet,

ancient Egyptian in style!..."
"They look to me like gnomes,
or silent sleeping queens
held in a magic spell..."

"You observe them, I suppose,
through all their various phases?"
"Yes, I meditate some pages
on these prisoners and their ways.

I observe from hour to hour;
my patience is extreme;
I shall write upon this theme
things never said before."

We observed those lives we found
mysterious, beautiful;
we discussed for quite a while
those chrysalids, spellbound.

But when a lock of her hair
tickled me on the face,
I turned about at once
and kissed her then and there.

I felt the soft percussion
of her heart, her precious hair
and all the windings there,
memory's intoxication...

Fine nostrils, learned mouth
I got to know, and yes,
commingled with her kiss,
the sharpness of her teeth,

that yielding to things as they seem,
that sly and gentle-seeming
glance, as of one who, dreaming,
wishes it were a dream...

19. *Another woman reborn*

Walking alone, like one who drifts around
aimlessly, and a little sad and tired,
I heard a hurried footstep on my right;
I recognised the shadow on the ground...
I shook like one expecting war; I turned
and, looking at her hair, saw it was white.

The meeting was a mournful one, not bitter.
We walked among the gold of the acacias,
crossing the Valentino close together.
She was discussing, tender and loquacious,
the past, herself, how times were now propitious,
the future, me, the brilliance of the weather.

"A beautiful November! Telling lies,
pretending to be spring! Yet listlessly
along these empty paths you take your way,
your face abstracted by your reveries...
Really you ought to act. You ought to seize
the thousand chances life presents today."

"The thousand chances... Futile fantasy!
Only abstracted from the vulgar herd
can I revive some dreams that I thought dead,
only relaxed when not in company...
Outside the town a great-aunt lives with me,
a mother who is sick, an uncle, mad.

I'm happy now. My life is made to fit
that dream which knows no shade of alteration:
to have a villa, living in seclusion;
by now without a past, without regret;
to be one's own man; think... I celebrate
exile and voluntary renunciation."

"Renounce renunciation with no name,
and leave both exile and oblivion
to me; resignedly I travel on,

82

the captive of our enemy, of Time...
You rise, my friend, towards a distant gleam!
I drop into a place whence light has gone!"

And she who talked to me was one who rose
out of the everlasting past! I found her
just on the tepid threshold of the winter!...
She was more beautiful by forty years,
with different beauty, sisterly, her eyes
tending to motherly and very tender.

I did not speak a word; I was spellbound:
that powerful profile still bewitches me;
her abundant hair was silver-shaded, and
she still looked young and fresh; she seemed to be
some goddess of the eighteenth century...
"Whatever are you thinking, lazy friend?"

"Of Petrarch overtaken on the road
by Laura, as I am by you..." And then
she smiled and laughed and showed her very fine
white teeth... "So I am Laura in the pride
of youth?... You're mocking me!... This hair of mine
is grey, you're thinking, now it isn't dyed."

20. *The frank refusal*

Deluded by my playful syllables,
you'll come perhaps to find my house deserted:
the number of the disappointed swells.
You're beautiful. You never hesitated
to offer me yourself. You are the undoubted
beautiful prey your open hand reveals.

Rather than seize you, with a firm and frank
gesture I stop you in the doorway, friend,
and, just as though you were a beggar, send
you on your way. I'm not the man you think!
I have to shout out this refusal frank-
ly so you will not curse me in the end.

I'm not the man I seem to you to be!
The man whom you consider a fraternal
spirit! My verse you know, tender and gay;
the heart inside is barren, shrill, and scornful,
an empty beanpod hanging in the mournful
blast of the north wind on a winter's day...

To keep you safe, lest my thoughts be impure,
my conscience has to hustle you away
in verses that are rather more sincere...
You are so beautiful; do not let me
see you: desire to seize the lovely prey
would make me feign the love you're hoping for.

I cannot love, and I have never loved
ever! That is the canker that I cover
up as I can. I've searched the wide world over
for love; in a sad pilgrimage I've lived
the past over again, a spoilt, depraved
child on the track of every vagrant pleasure...

So don't direct your little snow-white feet
to the dark soul of one who holds his peace!
Pale partisan, please do not tempt me thus!...
I'm not the man you think I am, despite
your dream (I ought to know, I fashioned it)!

You're curious over me. Leave me in peace!

21. *Turin*

How often in bright lands among bright flowers,
on shipboard, near the rigging, have my dreams
been only of your snows and sombre limes,
straight roads where tramlines glitter, and the ease
and elegance of your sharp milliners,
my city, well-disposed to happy times!

How often too, at night, exiled, my head
thrown back, I've dreamed beneath an open sky
of evenings in Turin, society
such as I love, drawing-rooms – bigoted,
Boeotian, gossipy – as in the good
Carlo Alberto's reign they used to be...

"...Count gets to know, he'll fix them in a rhyme..."
"Be quiet now..." – "It is a marvellous matter!..."
"You like la Duse?" – "I know little of her...
Well I, you see (no doubt she is sublime)
go to the theatre for a happy time..."
"Be quiet now!... Here comes the Reverend Father!..."

Very slowly a Barnabite comes up...
He presses the Contessa's hand – the loving
Contessa – and he seems to give his blessing...
The silent poet hardly glances up,
happy to find himself in such a group
with all the sadness of an old engraving.

He loves that barren world which shows no trace
of beauty, where they make a mockery
of Art. He loves that speech, those special ways,
that dull, disconsolate society.
He thinks of Giacomo, the marvellous boy,
the famous "hedge", the "savage native place".

II

As in an old Bavarian engraving
I see subalpine sky and setting sun...
From Palazzo Madama on and on
to the Valentino cloudy Alps are blazing...
This is Turin's *true* hour, this is the amazing,
the *venerable* hour of old Turin...

This is, I mean, the very best of hours
to think of the Risorgimento, and
young Massimo d'Azeglio, his *Memoirs*,
and being born too late... I would have found
life better with that tumult all around
than in this mild and dozy time of ours!

III

You have – rather provincial, démodé –
a certain chic that seems Parisian;
in you I see myself a child again,
I find once more my youthful easy way,
and you are dear as only she can be
who saw me come into the world, Turin!

Seeing me born you seemed to recognise
that absentminded youth must dream its dreams:
all of myself, all of my past pastimes,
my saddest and most tender memories
sleep sound in you, like camphorated clothes
buried away in cupboards in old rooms.

My earliest infancy...my time at school...
puberty...youth that longs to have its head...
my few and pallid loves...unsatisfied
suspense...boredom that's indescribable...
Death...and my Muse all by herself and all
disdainful, taciturn, misunderstood.

Although I follow many a wild chimera,
looking for somewhere else to settle down,
although I leave you, always moving on
down south to distant lands of heat and colour,
half of me stays with you, and I discover
myself again whenever I return.

I do return, because the heart is dark
and disappointed in its worldly pride.
You comfort me, for it was you who made
this soul so bourgeois with its light and dark:
Gianduia laughs and sobs, taken aback
if ever his horizons grow too wide...

Here's to the stick-in-the-muds... I do agree,
my wise Gianduia, Piedmont's puppet-clown!
A life without excitement is the one,
a life enjoying small things peacefully...

No point in getting roused... I do agree,
my wise Gianduia, Piedmont's puppet-clown!...

22. *In the survivor's home*

Out of a sky so gloomy it seems hope-
less drops the pleasant sleep-inducing snow,
wrapping, as they were spectres, all things up,
dropping, and reascending, sudden, slow,
down, up, now here, now there, it likes to throw
itself on windows and to tap, tap, tap...

Whirling in flakes as thick as cottonwool
it whitens all the roofs and muddy roads,
and bent boughs drop coagulated loads...
The fireplace has a crackle of live coal,
and the old veteran's remembering soul
under the sadness of such white subsides...

To him, the veteran of Love and Death,
they lied to him, those two fine things, they lied!
they lied to him, those two fine things, they lied:
there was no room for him upon Love's path,
and Death deceived him to the gates of Death,
poor rebel soul whose entrance was denied.

He fondles Makakita, his one friend;
she trembles with the dreadful chill of it,
presses against her poet, and takes fright
at what, outside the window and beyond,
monotonously stretches with no end,
involving everything in waves of white.

She thinks perhaps of woods where she was born,
the palmtrees, and the tamarinds, the miles
of tropic rivers, the quadrumanals –
her sisters – and her very favourite game:
hanging above the water in a chain,
prodding the nostrils of the crocodiles.

With Mummy near and with a peaceful heart
he loiters, hums an operatic air;
he sighs a little...manages to start
a hopeful flicker from the embers there...
He hums. He stops in front of Mummy dear
who knows, as Virgil did, unspoken thought.

He loiters, takes a photographic study
down from the piano: "Is this really me?"
He looks a long time at it fixedly,
seeing his former self distant already:
"Yes, I remember... Frivolous... And worldly...
Twenty-five nearly... What despondency!...

How comic the old self is and how mad!"
"What bitter sighs! What are you thinking of?"
"I'm thinking that I'll soon be twenty-five!
I'm ageing! Yet I'm still quite satisfied
with making verse! It's time to be the lad
with solemn thoughts his relatives approve.

That dream of art I found inspiring once
now fades; and I am slowly cured of it!
Far from the literati whom I hate,
in sober works, at moderate expense,
now may my paltry life at last evince
that there is bourgeois stuff in me all right..."

He sneers. He puts the photographic study
back on the piano: "Is this really me?"
He looks a long time at it fixedly,
seeing his former self distant already:
"Ailing a little... Frivolous... And worldly...
Yes, I remember... What despondency!..."

23. *Rain in August*

The sad wind knows no better than to wail,
and rain pours down; at first it merely scatters
drops in my garden; then it crackles, clatters
repeatedly in silvered single file...
I gaze upon the sodden Earth and feel
from time to time an onset of the jitters...

I know the pain of him who has to see
his sadness is in vain, no end in sight;
the water woven from immensity
tangles my dreaming in a kind of net,
and strange disquieting thin voices start
unsummoned from my great perplexity.

"Perplexity should think of taking wing
towards some end more vast and more remote!
Some noble faith should stir you into flight,
beyond yourself, to some Ideal Thing!
Look at your friends. Each one is quivering
as demagogue, believer, patriot...

Look at your friends. How they already place
their diverse faith in diverse schools of thought.
Not you. You sneer. Now what does your grimace
offer the anguished soul? What goal? What butt?
The Homeland? God? Humanity? Words that
the rhetoricians have made nauseous!...

Unsatisfied, the soul simply goes bad
in that clash of appetites, that brutal mix...
But question the old sorceress: she speaks
of how the one truth worth having can be had:
Nature! To put in verse, if one but could,
the mysteries she unveils to him who seeks!"

Nature, Mother Nature, is no deaf-mute;
if I consult with lichen, stocks and stones,
she shows her kindly purpose, makes no bones

about it, self-begotten, absolute,
the only truth not simply cut to suit,
in front of whom all sneering stops at once.

She comforts with good hope my miserable
youth that I spend so very much alone;
the dandelion seed that flies wind-blown,
the flint, the blindworm, and the swallow-tail
are characters to me, *personae*; all
preserve for me a language of their own...

The heart that once has heard them finds no peace
in pallid visions fading very fast;
far other springs and objects are its choice...
O my mild Muse, who think silence is best
when copy-cats are wailing fit to burst,
I'll come back poet with another voice!

24. *The colloquies*

These *Colloquies*… Now sound of body and mind,
he groups his verses and he alters them,
weighing the manuscript with even hand.

– A bit of fun with syllables and rhyme:
is this what stays of my so fleeting spring?
Is it all really here, my youthful prime?

Better be silent, calmly vanishing
now while my garden still shows signs of life,
and envy still is unprovoked to sting.

Better upon life's road to stop for breath,
now while the world to my inexpert Muse –
an actress sadly singing of her youth –

holds out a helping hand or gives applause.

II

This Muse of mine's no actress full of years
who paints her face and goes on like a child,
however much the mob derides and jeers;

young she will hold her tongue, still undefiled
by Time, like that Contessa Castiglione,
so beautiful, of whom such tales are told.

Who, finding her spring day not quite so sunny,
her youth begin to fade, sealed up the doors,
and stayed a sort of prisoner with only

Time for companion, waiting for the years
in rooms with tattered hangings, mirrorless,
hiding from common folk and courtiers

her decadence, the ultimate disgrace.

As for my image, I want it to stay
twenty, as in a portrait, never altered;
my friends, you will not see me on my way

bent by the years and tremulous and battered!
In this my silence I shall stay the friend
who was so dear to you, a touch dim-witted;

I'll be that youngster still, old-fashioned, fond,
who sighed with longing in the light of stars,
Artur and Friedrich always on his mind,

and yet forsook rebel philosophers
to give the swallow its due sepulchre
or reach a blade of grass towards the claws

of topsyturvy coleoptera...

LETTERS

1
To Don Fausto Graziani

Savigliano, 5 June 1903

The forthcoming ceremony which will consecrate you for ever could not correspond more to my state of mind: and this letter will not merely be a few polite lines, but best wishes from an atheist friend to a friend who is a believer, because – as you know – I do not believe. All the same, never before did I realise the heroism of your vocation, all the sacred poetry which goes with it. You know the passion which I have for literature; I have read a great deal and learned a great deal, not in the barren classrooms of the grammar school, but on my own account, raising myself, I do feel, high above my companions who live unconscious of vulgarity: I have read a great deal and become passionately fond of all those poets who have celebrated pleasure and life, from the Greek Mimnermus to our own very modern Gabriele d'Annunzio: all names which to you, who are ministers of God, will sound infamous and satanic. And yet – would you believe it? – Gabriele d'Annunzio, that very person who celebrated the *Pleasure* to be obtained from all kinds of lust and depravity, has instilled into my mind a mystical sense which I used not to have. I saw him in his masterpieces drawing attention to the names and sayings of several mystics of the Church and I was pricked with curiosity to know them more closely. With this in mind I went the rounds of the libraries, with this in mind I got hold of the works of Saint Francis of Assisi, of Saint Clare, of Saint Catherine of Siena, and so bit by bit I got to know the souls of these Blessed Ones. Of course my thirst is only the thirst of the artist who finds in those ancient writings a beauty indicative of deep things; all the same on my writing-desk now, next to the *Three hundred positions* of Pietro Aretino are the epistles of Saint Clare, next to *Pleasure* is the volume of letters by Saint Catherine of Siena. For several months I have been immersed in those texts and (I swear that what I say is the simple truth) all the hours my studies leave free I devote to meditating on those most ancient books; I am completely won over by them, but faith has not on that account come down into my heart; in me it is only the admiration of the artist which speaks. I admire the heroism of the "Poor man of Assisi", who against his father's will renounced the fashionable way of life which his easy circumstances would have allowed him, in order to go and preach, poor and barefoot, the brotherhood of all things. I have read the Canticle of the Sun so many times that now I have it by heart, and the harmonious hymn of

97

the man from Assisi haunts my mind, as the memory of a beautiful symphony haunts the ear.

> Be praised, my Lord, with all your creatures
> especially His Highness Brother Sun
> who is the light of day and you give us light by him;
> of You Most High he bears witness.
> Be praised, my Lord, for sister moon and the stars.
> Be praised, my Lord, for brother wind.
> Be praised, my Lord, for sister water
> who is very useful and humble and precious and chaste.
> Be praised, my Lord, for brother fire,
> by whom you illuminate the night for us
> and he is handsome and most vigorous and strong.
> Be praised, my Lord, for our sister mother earth...
> Be praised, my Lord, for our sister bodily death...

Oh Fausto, I think only Dante could compete with this poetry, so spontaneous and sincere: poetry which to the mob is probably unintelligible and perhaps even ridiculous, but which you certainly will understand. And I wish you, Fausto, in your most arduous vocation a zeal like that which kept Saint Francis of Assisi on the mountains of La Verna at the approach of the Feast of the Exaltation of the Holy Cross; that zeal which made the Saint worthy of the stigmata when he, redoubling his fasting and prayers, saw one morning, coming on the rays of the rising sun from the farthest limits of the horizon, a Seraph nailed to a cross; and the heart of the Blessed One endured at that sight such grief and such pleasure that there remained in his hands the true marks of the Passion of Our Lord Jesus Christ. Auto-suggestion or miracle? I certainly do not know, but – note this – while writing these mystical recollections down for you my artistic intellect trembles inexplicably... Now what must your believing heart not experience in reading of such treasures, when my atheist soul is moved by them? * * *

In a month I have the ordeal of my diploma and now I am in a state of anxious expectation, but if I pass my examinations, this summer in the peace and quiet of Il Meleto I want to meditate at length on the volumes of the medieval mystics. Do not think because of this, however, that the hour of grace has come down into me: that would necessitate my putting my forefinger into the bleeding wound: and will your prayers be so ardent as to renew for your atheist friend the miracle of Saint Thomas? I do not dare to hope it. * * *

2
To Amalia Guglielminetti
San Giuliano d'Albaro, 26 May 1907

For two days I shall deny myself the pleasure of writing to you.

That is because my Mother is here on the beach – she arrived yesterday unexpectedly, and she will leave again tomorrow evening. So I shall not go up to the inn again to write a letter which for me is too inviting and which will not be brief.

But I wish to thank you straightaway for the volume *which I have now received* and which by now I have had in my possession since the 19th (the dates of my trips to Genoa, in this enforced solitude, are unforgettable!). And perhaps the copy sent to me out of friendship has been held back by my sister in Turin; and I am happy about that.

I have read your book.

And some friends (Giuseppe De Paoli, among others) read it to me again yesterday morning on the crossing from San Giuliano to Portofino: your volume travelled with us, on an old fishing-boat (and you did not know!). Rossi read aloud: and your rhymes had a coil of rope as a lectern and the sea as a commentary. And you did not know! * * *

3
To Amalia Guglielminetti
San Giuliano d'Albaro, 5 June 1907

First of all, please excuse my delay.

I have been ill – or rather, worse than that, I have been ill for several months. Today, the second day that I have felt better, I have read your verses again for the fifth or sixth time, from beginning to end.

And in order straightaway to rid a letter like this of the usual trite phrases, *I swear to you*, dear Signorina, that in the whole of Italian literature written by women, past or present, I do not know any work of poetry comparable to yours.

The "worthy garland" of sonnets which you have succeeded in fashioning, gives you the very first place, not among women (among women you have no competition: *women do not know how to write*) but among the most promising masculine talents. * * *

This whole work of yours is organic: at whatever page one opens the little volume, one is conscious of the scent of the same garden; the garden where you walk leading by the hand a train of

99

companions. And the reader has the impression of being admitted for a few moments into a cloistral garden: at every turn of the path, among the clusters of lilies and the overarching roses, another band of virgins appears in front of him, celebrating a new kind of martyrdom or hope. In your book you almost achieve what Virgil did, guiding the reader through the rings of that shining Inferno which is called virginity. You have known how to ennoble and raise into a primal ideal that figure – oppressed, ambiguous, often derided – which in our days takes the name of Signorina. Signorina – what an ugly word! A worthy product of the evolutionary stage we have reached, which even of the virgin has made a creature who is oppressed and indeterminate, like that ugly name: *Signorina.* * * *

Signorina: a figure of sadness; or else one who, unconscious of her distress, perhaps lives supremely happy, intellectually impoverished by age-old bourgeois narrow-mindedness, or who, consciously revolting against the "wisdom of the ancient standards", seeks for herself and her sisters a way of salvation, or who, even more rebellious, wishes to be free to claim a destiny for herself and dispute it with scornful men, or who languishes in the dream of hopeless expectation. * * *

And the signorina who is passionate! She is, among us, another figure again, one whom the world regards with a feeling of sardonic pity. You have probably noticed it too. People are more touched, they almost have more indulgent charitable sympathy with the vicissitudes of an adulterous relationship than with the fortunes of a virginal idyll. That is how literature wishes it to be: and it is literature that shapes life. * * *

4
To Amalia Guglielminetti
San Giuliano d'Albaro, 10 June 1907

Thank you for the letter, and special thanks for some truths that the letter contains.

I remember that winter evening at the Cultural Society, and I am glad to talk about it.

My goodness! At what a silly time you surprised me (surprised: because I only noticed your presence when the conversation had gone on for a long while); I beg you, however, to notice I was not talking, but rather they were making me talk! It was that lady and gentleman who were making me talk, clothing me too with discourtesy: and the rather derisory harshness of my voice was caused precisely and solely by them – by the man above all, who was quite a philistine… In addition my agitation grew when I noticed, holding aloof, your silent and hostile figure.

Hostile: for a long time I had known I was antipathetic to you: perhaps even before you knew it yourself… Like all those men who profess vanity and flirtatiousness (you see that I make my confession wretchedly!) I have a quick and infallible intuition which forebodes and brings to my notice what the opinion of the ladies is. Moreover, one evening you too were discourteous to me. On behalf of the management, I was going the rounds of the Cultural Society, inviting the members to give their signatures for a purchase.

It came to the turn of you and your sister; I approached civilly; civilly I begged your pardon for distracting you from the reading, I offered you the pen: you added your signature. Then, when I thought I ought to tell you my name, you leapt to your feet with a gesture of indignant surprise such as I was not able and would not be able to define: a gesture which reminds me of the rebellious pride of certain of your sonnets. And – more discourteous – you did this so as not to offer me your hands: one of them you held behind your back, in order to twist the chair round, and the other you imprisoned, wrapping it three times in your boa, a large boa of black feathers I think.

I was antipathetic to you: I am not surprised.

Women always find me antipathetic, before they know me. (Let us not speak about men: they detest me and I detest them; I have no friends. And even my dearest friends are women).

Women always find me antipathetic; but later they love me. You too will love me.

And you? Do you think that I find you very congenial? You have rather, to my eyes, some qualities which are off-putting.

First of all you are beautiful.

And beautiful in exactly the way I like. I have seen little of you, but observed a great deal: you are really beautiful (I swear that I am annoyed, almost, to have to admit it so stupidly!).

I have studied you a great deal. I have never been able to find out, for example, whether, beneath the huge plumed helmets, in the style of Rembrandt, which you favour, your hair is parted in the old style or not; but I have strongly impressed on my mind how your hair is wavy at the temples and how it is gathered in a supple knot at the back of your neck.

I also have in mind this: that you have beautiful teeth and a beautiful mouth, rather large and fresh and attractive as few are, and that you have two beautiful eyes (even this I have to admit, and almost with annoyance) two eyes of a servile gentleness: the eyes of her who yields to her despotic lord and offers him her feverish wrists and looks at them encircled with chains, almost enjoying it; you also have the profile I like, you dress as I like and you walk as I like – with the rather weary and absentminded elegance of our greatest actress... You see that there was enough to make me shun your acquaintance. Not indeed that I was afraid of falling in love with you (*I have only ever fallen in love with myself;* I mean: with that which goes on in myself) but I was afraid that I might like you: that was all. Added to that, there was the literary fame which – before the *Foolish virgins* – gave me an indefinable sense of aversion – from any woman writer – from Corinna to Ada Negri... An example? One time...but no! I cannot tell you: woe betide me if I indulge in fraternal sincerity: I shall become *discourteous*... You positively wish to know? So be it! But I take no responsibility, mind, and I shall reconstruct the dialogue verbatim for you. On one occasion, last year, we – Vallini, Bassi, Vugliano, and others – were in the room where the newspapers are, you – alone – in the one with the magazines, standing, upright, with your arm stretched out, leafing through the reviews on the table. And among us this is more or less what was being said:

– She is beautiful.
– Yes, she is beautiful!
– But she writes.
– And not badly. * * *
– Who is that D.M. who introduces her work?
– Dino Mantovani.
– He compares her to Gaspara Stampa and to Sappho...
– He must know her.
– Evidently: I bet he's paying court to her.
– And she?
– And she, like all women, perhaps permits it just enough so that she can make use of him when necessary.
– But is it certain?
– Not certain. I'm guessing. But it is reasonable to infer it. For us who are not young ladies, there is no critic who would make every effort like that.
– And she is a very respectable lady from a very good family...
– They certainly say that she is respectable.
– She is, she is: I guarantee it: I know the family.
– What a pity!
– What is?
– That she is a young lady.

102

– And that she is respectable.
– What a pity: she is really beautiful!
– If only she were illiterate.
– But she writes!
– Women who write really are detestable!
– If they write badly they annoy us.
– If they write well they humiliate us.
– Shut up! She's coming this way.

And you, my Friend, passed among us, proud dignified tranquil. But certainly as you passed you sensed something which displeased you; like a certain hostility – (no: hostility is too much) – but an indefinable coldness; and in the air you still felt there was something unfavourable, ironically petty and vulgar (as all of us men are petty and vulgar, deep down. All of us: do not deceive yourself). I have put this recollection into dialogue-form for you, my friend, in order to define that indefinable feeling which was separating us and which you sensed and which I sensed: it was the surroundings, the vulgar irony of the surroundings.

On the other hand, now that we are distant from each other – I seriously ill and exiled from the city for two or three years: perhaps more – we are well able to be friends. You have spoken to me about us corresponding. Most certainly! But I wish to be honest right from the start, as tradesmen do: I am not a spiritual friend: I am at best a mediocre cerebral interlocutor... I do not believe in the soul and I have a deep contempt for my spirit and yours, to which I do not attach any more importance than to the energy which moves an earthworm and the chlorophyll which colours a stalk of grass: and that very song of yours, so disdainful even in passion, so high and pure and chaste, is only the cry of your agitated modesty, shrinking under the lash of instinct, of that instinct which provides for the continuation of the species... Do you accept as a friend a man who says this to you?

Be warned that my way of thinking will lead me sometimes to write to you things of a coarseness such as to border on impropriety... Will you be so highminded as to forgive me?

And start to forgive me for the prolixity of this letter – we are on the third sheet of paper, I think! – Today my friends from Genoa were here, as they often are, journalists and poets, all soulmates and all ill of our same illness, my good Friend.

We went on a boat, as usual, we recited verses, as usual, and we also, an unaccustomed pleasure, had a good blow-out on bananas and medlars. We let ourselves drift all the day, until it was twilight, on a sea the colour of nothing, so that we seemed to be flying.

I recited, and without the book, several of your sonnets: I think I know about fifteen by heart, perfectly and without having studied them. Little by little I shall absorb the whole volume. * * *

5
To Giulio De Frenzi
Agliè Canavese, 28 June 1907

* * * All the doctors (from Maragliano to Pescarolo) swear that I only have a bronchial inflammation in its early stages at the top of the left lung. In fact I have no troubles of any kind: but only disquieting symptoms: a cough, insomnia, a slight fever, saliva streaked with little veins of blood...all the symptoms which banish the desire to celebrate *unserious things*; the scorn of rhetoricians and my only delight! Celebrate serious things? I am afraid that is not my forte. So you liked the verses in the *Rassegna*? I am glad. I have quite a collection of verses of that kind, written and to be written; I shall complete it gradually, in the various resorts I visit in my exile. But how kind you were to me in that article of yours in the *Carlino*! You have taken me seriously and have treated my *Way of refuge* as a respectable person! It is too much. My good friends wrote to me at San Giuliano with perspicacious zeal to say that I should not deceive myself and that beneath your over-exaggerated eulogy was hidden a trace of irony and scorn. The clearsightedness of friendship! And they know that I am ill and that a little self-deception sometimes helps more than creosote and quinine! In you, on the other hand, who fortunately are not one of my friends, I am conscious of a sincere and brotherly kindness, and it is for this, more than for the too-strong flattery, that I am so grateful to you!

I shall send you this autumn, if you wish, some of my new unpublished verses: who would ever have said that I would woo the tubercular Muse! The Muse of good old Lorenzo Stecchetti! I have reread, after years and years, the precious little volume... But how obvious it is that the Poet had completely healthy lungs! The thought of dying is quite a different thing, quite a different thing! There one is: I could not say how. But one does not grumble, or curse, or say nasty things. One waits for death with a smile: one is almost well. * * *

104

6
To Amalia Guglielminetti

I am a clod – there is no other word for it – but I am also a sick man and a sick man who for some time has been worse. So forgive me then!

Please believe that when *certain symptoms* reappear the spirit falls into such certainty about the probable truth that it longs for a quick end... And that thing which is called Earth, with the sea the continents the rivers the trees the mountains the houses the men, is already distant: and even friends disappear too: even the most dear; and even you among them. Now that it is some days since hope was born again (I recognise by now this alternation of times of respite) your face reappears and your friendship is once more pleasant to me. * * *

7
To Marino Moretti
Ceresole Reale, 27 July 1907

* * * Thank you for your kind expression of affection, which I reciprocate cordially. For us, who are dreamers, all ill with the same illness (to me poetry is a sickness), nothing remains but to give each other a helping hand and go on together. * * *

8
To Amalia Guglielminetti
Ceresole Reale, 3 August 1907

* * * For several weeks I have been here in delightful solitude and with a scenario in front of me that brings to mind the second act of *The daughter of Iorio*... Yes really! I have no Mila for companion, but a maidservant who comes from this part of the world and is very prosaic. She does not bore me, however: in the evening, while I contemplate the sunset on the snow-covered peaks of the Levanne, she talks. I do not pay any attention to her: but her voice reaches me from time to time, through the rumble of my melancholy, and I grasp some snatches of fine things, episodes which I shall perhaps exploit in my poetry: "The tale of the parish priest who ran away with the daughter of the mayor" or else "The marchesa who fell in love with the guide; and they were

surprised by the husband". And so on...

But do not think ill of us, my Friend! She is a most virtuous girl, the daughter of Maria, and I cherish for her the most respectful repugnance: picture to yourself a body which is eighteen years old, but which in the city would be despised by an old woman of eighty, picture to yourself a face which is square, pale, pink, freckled, without pupils, without eyelashes, without eyebrows, with sticky yellow hair drawn back, drawn back smoothly tightly and closely at the back of the neck in a bunch of very tiny plaits, and spread all over the face the signs of hereditary idiocy... and this is she who will be my servant until my Mother arrives from the seaside. * * *

My health is relatively better. But just think – for months I have been wearing an inhaler mask, day and night, and this contrivance, enclosing almost all my face in a metal mesh, gives me the stupid look of a diver.

It does, however, make me much better: and almost all the disturbing symptoms have disappeared under the continual force of the powerful essence of balsam.

Ah! Health! Health! What a marvellous thing! One can jump, laugh, bawl, pay court to beautiful ladies!

But this winter I may get better!

And what a dreadful nostalgia I feel for ladies who are well-dressed, well-shod, well-coiffured... What a longing to embrace a beautiful ensemble of perfect cut! Ah! Shepherdesses and the countryside are not for me... And yet for some time longer I shall have to put up with them if I value my life... Write to me, write to me, and also confide in me a little: are you much courted? Among the many men who pay court to you, someone is less stupid than the others, and you like him most?

I must leave you, because this contrivance on my nose destroys the co-ordination of my eyes and forces me to follow the pen now with one eye, now with the other: as a hen would... Pity me.

9
To Giulio De Frenzi
Ceresole Reale, 3 August 1907

Do not call me *ungrateful* (in this instance I would only be *ill-advised*: with a favourable judge like yourself...) but I have no verses to send you! I have only a mass of raw material which will need patient elaboration before it is presentable. You are the one I particularly do not wish to disappoint, after what you have thought of me. Meanwhile, thanks to your good humour and that of your friends, my little volume – abandoned for months to the integrity (shall we call it that) of the publishers – is in its third edition!

My health. Not bad. The infection which worries me most seems to be allowing itself to yield to the cure, to the most fastidious magic formulae. I hope to patch it up properly! Meanwhile, for months, I have been wearing the mask continuously, day and night, and I feel that it really is a help; only I believe that it is to this continual inspiration of strong essences that I owe the sleepiness, the cerebral inertia which I have noticed for some time. How very different from Graf! I feel myself becoming dafter day by day, on my word of honour! And yet after your judgements in the best journals, I am obliged to be an intelligent person! I don't know quite what to do… The only remedy is silence.

Certainly I shall not publish very soon, not in under two years: who knows what the devil you are demanding from me, all you who have sweetened my first appearance! If you knew how this thought weighs me down! I am almost ready to beg you to take back your too-kind reviews!

I am joking, my dear De Frenzi, and I have rather such trust in your friendship that I shall perhaps send you (when it is in existence) a little booklet of my things; and so on, from time to time, until after some years there will be such a mass of them that I shall be able to sift them strictly and extract from them a volume that will be brief but choice.

I leave you. If you knew what an effort I have to make to write! With this contrivance on the nose, which destroys the co-ordination of my eyes, I have to follow the pen now with one eye now with the other, as a hen would. * * *

10
To Amalia Guglielminetti
Rivarolo Canavese, 4 October 1907

I am very happy!

So I shall expect you (from Wednesday onwards, since I have to stay here until then) and my Mother will expect you too, for she is a reader and a great admirer of yours. In fact, on her behalf and not on my own behalf, for that would be "unbecoming") I entreat you earnestly to devote the whole day to your evangelical pilgrimage. And I approve the idea, even though having lunch together makes a terribly bourgeois beginning to a friendship like ours...

It will be a very sensible and hardly romantic meeting: such as certainly would not have been dreamed of by two poets of the last century: but you are not George Sand and I am not Alfred de Musset. * * *

11
To Amalia Guglielminetti
Agliè Canavese, 23 October 1907

* * * Here I am again in this solitude and once more far from well. The indisposition of which I was complaining on that day, and which made it hard for me to speak and almost painful to connect my thoughts, has still not left me. I feel a lassitude in my bones, and an emotional haze in my brain, both of which I find truly humiliating!

My dear good Friend, I should like to be in your drawingroom once again and hold, as medicine, your hands in my hands, and stay like that, without saying anything, just looking at you: *"playing with glances is a charming thing..."* You certainly know how to look: so much so that, from our meetings, the silences stay in my mind almost more than the words. And that is natural: between us two it is almost impossible to discuss deep and serious things by word of mouth: I as much as you have a mind too corroded by irony to keep up a staid discussion seriously for very long. Because of this – and also because of my physical prostration – our last conversation was rather empty, made up of repeated trivialities and bits of gossip, like an ordinary meeting of ordinary people.

And we are not ordinary people! * * *

Your beauty! I feared it so much! That day at Il Meleto I was annihilated by it: I considered it a terrible enemy to the seriousness of our friendship. Only the other day I was trying to demolish it, by dint of analysis and sophistry, but in vain! * * *

12
To Amalia Guglielminetti
Agliè Canavese, 12 November 1907

* * * I am better in health, my friend, I am much better (I know that you love me and that this will please you). I am better also because I am in love! With a lady who does not exist, of course!

Signorina Domestica.

A delightful provincial creature, who wears no face-powder and no corset, she has a square face and a masculine jaw, a little snub nose covered with pale freckles, and two clear eyes without eyebrows, as in Flemish paintings; do not laugh, my friend!

You will meet my Beauty again among the smells of roasted coffee, of lavender, of stamped official paper, and of ink gone bad; with in the background a tapestry showing rococo lozenge-shaped garlands, each enclosing a separate episode of the pitiable fable of Pyramus and Thisbe... It is strange that I should be thus cerebrally enamoured of such a person, when I can still see you in my mind's eye, the very image of a modern refined woman. Perhaps it is a reaction, a beneficial reaction...

I did want to write a piece of prose about her, with short lyrical chapters, united by an emotional plot, chaste, pure, healthy, like the flesh of the protagonist: but I shall probably not do it.

Every time that I set about doing it I am overcome by a loss of willpower, a trembling, a verbal and metrical impotence, all of them indefinable...

These are troubles which you too will certainly recognise, troubles which come upon us in the act of translating into tangible appearances a dream we have dreamed for too long. I shall perhaps make it into a poem, but, I very much fear, a mediocre one. * * *

13
To Amalia Guglielminetti
San Giuliano d'Albaro, 9 December 1907

My poor Friend, I have the sea in front of me and you are not there any more! What a strange thing! One says goodbye to a creature, one boards a train, one goes, one goes, one gets off, one looks around: and the creature is no longer there! She is no longer there: it is as if she were dead: all that remains of her in the mind's eye are some of her gestures, some notes of her voice, nothing else. What a strange thing!

And I have seen the sea again, the sea which can console us for so many things, even for this last wicked day of ours...

On my return, here in the very place where I received your first letters, my spirit has gone back to the time when you were still for me "Amalia Guglielminetti".

And everything that Destiny wished to make of us seems to me the spasm of someone in a fever; and of the wickedness no more remains than a rather pungent sweetness on the lips and gums, as when the corolla of certain sweet violets has been chewed too long...

And yet the sea is always the great purifier: I feel that my spirit is light and spotless, as though it were born only yesterday! There is a warmth, a gaiety in the air! All the horizon which can be seen from my window is but the harmony of two blue bands: one darker: the sea; one brighter: the sky – I am writing to you as best I can, my friend! I am almost on my knees on a little chair with the paper on a book and the book on the chest of drawers: I still have no writing desk!

But there is the sea outside...

I shudder at the thought that you might see me like this, you who suffer so much from vulgar things!

I am uncombed, bearded, dressed in a coarse jersey and a tattered jacket: I broke the nail of my little finger when opening a suitcase and my finger is disgustingly encrusted with blood...

But there is the sea outside!

My room is cheerless, with lime-washed walls, with wretched furnishings, cluttered here and there with my untidy luggage: books, boxes, medicine bottles, suits, underclothes; a small flask of inhalant has fallen open during the journey and the stuff is spreading through the room, with the smell of floor polish, a very keen smell.

I have a thousand humiliating little things to provide with my own hands: boiling water for the inhalations, boiling water for the eggs (there is no way to make the cook understand how I want them boiled), making coffee for myself (just imagine!), tidying the drawers, presiding over the care of the linen...

But there is the sea outside: and I am happy! I stoop to all these material things which at home I know nothing about, and I am happy!

Leaving Turin I had something like a feeling of liberation. On account of so many things. And principally on account of you.

It was time!

It was time to put between the two of us many months and kilometres! Not indeed that I was about to commit some act o madness (I have unfortunately never loved yet and perhaps shall not love any more; I shall never love if I have not loved you!), but the desire for your person was starting to inflame my blood in a dreadfully cruel way; the notion of coupling a desperate and sharp pleasure with the spiritual beauty of a superior intelligence like yours now turns out to be humiliating to me, monstrous, unbearable...

110

When the other day I went out from your drawingroom with the first impression of your mouth on my mouth it seemed to me that I had profaned something in us, something of much more value than that brief spasm of our young nerves, I seemed to see scattered in one moment of forgetfulness a treasure accumulated with an effort, over such a long time, by both of us.

And the day before yesterday, when you got out with your dress and your hat and your hair all rumpled, and left me alone in that common cab, I fell back completely exhausted against the seat, where your exquisite perfume was being succeeded by the pungent smell of the torn leather... And during the return drive (dreadful!) homewards I felt the blood rushing through my veins and striking me on the back of my neck like a sledgehammer, and, to the noisy rhythm of the windows' rattle, I felt once more on my mouth the cruelty of your eye-teeth. I went back into the house with but one desire: to go away, to leave Turin immediately.

And today I have the sea in front of me!

I am free and I am happy.

I wrote to you days ago that in this peace your image would be revived in my memory, "like the frond in the water when it's calm again" – It is true! Already you have returned to me as the good sister who – when you were near to me – "you did not feel yourself to be" –.

I am going to look at the sea before I say goodbye to you.

The sea is raging: it is crumpling under my window and boiling up with a hollow voice... It has not said goodbye to me and it does not let me say goodbye to you.

I think, looking at it and listening to it, of an irate judge who is issuing a warning to both of us. * * *

14
To Amalia Guglielminetti
San Giuliano d'Albaro, 11 December 1907

* * * I am writing to you on the beach, sitting on the pier where in summer the beach-huts are set out. I am writing to you with the paper laid on my working portfolio and the portfolio on my knees... How well I am! I am happy! I wish for nothing, I do not wish for you, I do not wish for my Mother, I do not wish for friends... I let myself live... It is so pleasant! I have your pensive portrait (thanks!) pressed in the pages of the book which I am reading: "The sensitive plant" by P.B. Shelley. I am rereading everything by that great young man; and no place is more worthy for such a

111

reading than this Dantean rocky beach, with in front of it the sea, that same sea where the *heart of hearts* stopped beating...

What a dreadful sea! So it must have been on that memorable day. I see the waves coming from a distance, from the farthest horizon, coming nearer, coming nearer and nearer, bending over, crowning themselves with foam, and breaking into a seething mass... Every tenth time, a wave arrives which is bolder than the others and I have to retreat to save my book and papers from the eddy. And there is a pleasant smell of salt and seaweed and iodine which I breathe in deep into my chest...

I want to get better!

Life is still beautiful, for anyone who has the sense not to take part in it, to *save himself* in time. On account of this I bless my illness which imposes this exile on me, body and soul. * * *

15
To Amalia Guglielminetti
San Giuliano d'Albaro, 23 December 1907

* * * I have roughed out a poem, in hendecasyllables and sestinas; the poem is fine, the lines are ugly. It is a recollection of a *cocotte* whom I knew at Cornigliano Ligure, almost twenty years ago (in 1889: I was five years old!). She was our next-door neighbour, since she was renting for the bathing the other half of the villa which we were renting. But our garden and hers were divided by a railing: and it was through the bars that she hugged me sometimes saying to me *"Mon petit chéri!"* with a smile which I still remember, a smile in which all the nostalgia of her unsatisfied maternal instinct was weeping. Then my family noticed her, they spoke of her at the table, I heard from my mother the word cocotte... * * *

From that year I have never again seen my French friend, the wicked Signorina. On the other hand, I have seen Cornigliano again, last week, and the garden of twenty years ago, and I felt a great need of her. * * *

16
To Amalia Guglielminetti
San Giuliano d'Albaro, 6 January 1908

I take refuge with you, after three hours of dreadful correspondence: four letters, nine postcards, endless greetings cards: all

112

the epistolary arrears of a week and more.

How tired I am and how in a fraternal way I must love you, if I dare to throw down these words, ill-controlled because of my tiredness, in a letter to you, so good certainly, but also so sensitive to disharmony!

How are you, how are you, my dear Amalia?

As for me, for some days I have not been so well. I have had a very painful bout of neuralgia and I am rather dazed by the phenacetin and the quinine... But it will pass! The sky and the sea are so marvellously propitious. I am writing to you, as always, with the window wide open, and every time I lift my eyes from the pen I see in the azure rectangle some ships making for who knows where! And my thoughts start to fade away, I follow with my eyes a white seagull which is disappearing with its wings spread: I too disappear, I am lost... Then I see the sheet of paper again, your image reappears to me as if in sorrowful reproof: how soon one forgets! I am forgetting you, Amalia! I am forgetting you (I must explain) *physically*. It is an odd sort of anguish, which gives a true sense of our great cerebral poverty: I cannot succeed any longer, however much I try, in remembering certain small details of your face, of your hands...

The oval of your face is gradually fading, the exact shade of your hair is changing, the arch of your eyebrows is being distorted: I remember little of your chin and hardly any more of your ear (which must be beautiful, however, if I praised it on one occasion). And in such incipient decay the eyes and mouth remain lively and they survive, too strongly impressed on my mind and lips to be forgotten...

But in this slow disappearance your spiritual image (you ask me about it in your last letter) is more clearly defined, it leaps to mind, its contours precise: I love you very much, my dear Amalia! And you are to me the true *friend*, the companion of dreams and of sadness. The moments of youthful error which enthralled both of us are already forgotten (the Sea cancels and wears away very different things!) and I feel myself already alien, immune to your physical attraction, free from all sensual slavery. * * *

17
To Amalia Guglielminetti
San Giuliano d'Albaro, 15 January 1908

* * * I have set your small portrait (the other, the large one, is not on display) in the frame of the mirror. A few moments ago

I scratched your left hand out with a pin, because the camera-angle had made it look huge.

I chose to maim you. Did your left hand not hurt a few moments ago? (It is 3.20 p.m. on Wednesday). * * *

18
To Amalia Guglielminetti
Turin, 21 March 1908

* * * Amalia, I feel, I swear to you that we shall soon have arrived and that we shall give to the world and the world will give to us what is owed to us: and one day, meeting each other, we shall be proud of having, in a distant time of madness, come across each other on the road. From a bond like ours something more worthy than the paltry sentimentality of petty lovers should leap into prominence. For this it is necessary that we should not see each other again. We shall not see each other again for a long time, my good friend Amalia, for many months, for some years perhaps. Because I want it to be like this.

And it will be easy for me. I am leaving Turin within days, I shall pass the spring in the Canavese, the summer in the mountains, the autumn at Il Meleto (you will not come to visit me), the winter and spring in Liguria...and for two years it will not be obvious that I am a native of Turin. I had rather not see you again until then.

We shall still be young and we shall still love each other.

We shall love each other even more, because we shall be wearied by fresh disappointments in the meantime, and perhaps, looking at each other's eyes and mouth, we shall still shiver. Or else we shall not shiver any more, and you will be another's. I shall not suffer.

How long it is since I suffered! I fear I shall not be able to suffer any more: I feel a disturbing calm come down into my soul, I feel my facial muscles relax in the serene composure of a placid mask...

I must confess to you that my soul is rather alarmed by this...

Whatever may be the fate which destiny has in store for us, we shall always be friends, great friends who are necessary to each other like two travellers who follow the same road and hold each other by the hand. * * *

114

19
To Amalia Guglielminetti

Turin, 30 March 1908

Every day I reread your letter, my good friend Amalia, with great melancholy. And I delay my answer, since I am taken with a painful indolence: perhaps because I do not know very well how to tell you...

For many days I have been inside the house and I am morbidly drowsy, uncertain of everything as though I were in a dream.

I think about so many things, above all those in the future; and I think also of you, with much tenderness and with much serenity.

I feel in the depths of my soul a sort of proud sadness, because I have managed to be cruel with myself and perhaps – forgive me – also a little with you...

I experience a particular satisfaction whenever I refuse some great happiness which Destiny offers me.

And what happiness, my Friend!

Our love which would have flowered with all the flowers of the spring in Turin! (So sweet for the exile who returns!) Even the season would have favoured our folly!

And how many months of serenity, of sun, of scent! And how many dreams! We would have liked to wander with our passion through all the surroundings which are favourable to sentiment: how many dreams! I have already dreamed them all and seen you already in all of them: with in the background the unknown countryside, the country lanes where at my side the outline of your svelte Parisian figure would have been.

I shall not see your new clothes. I shall be far off, alone, with my taciturn ambition: a companion much more cruel than your melancholy... Why should I not confess it to you, my good sister?

For some time ambition has had hold of me in a terrible manner.

I do not feel I do not see I do not enjoy I do not endure anything else. How can you, when you hold in your hands the seeds of a thousand hopes and follow the same path as myself, how can you still direct your youthful powers to other destinies? For me, striding straight on, with my eyes fixed on my distant goal (how distant it is!), everything else is minor and negligible: joys and griefs: everything, even your beauty over which I have bent for one instant, as over a flower at the side of the path, but which I am promptly leaving behind, because it would delay my peaceful steps for too long... Ah! If I could give you only a part of this latent pride of mine, even the suffering which you say you have within you would pale into insignificance, and love would appear

115

to you as it is: a youthful deception and a negligible episode in a destiny like mine and yours. And never before as at this time, when such a frenzy makes me suffer, have I had such contempt for my artistic abilities and felt so much the need to refine them with study, meditation, and silence. You are still eager to pluck flowers and enjoy the passing hour: to me even the allurement of pleasure is intolerable, since it is an obstacle on my path.

Amalia, my good friend, how many things like this I would say to you and I would wish to say to you if you were not young and beautiful! But you have bright eyes and a tempting mouth and it is impossible to be near you without becoming irreverent towards you as though you were some milliner or courtesan...

I have reread these six pages, my friend: alas! I talk, I talk, and, above all, I argue: how I must be making you suffer! And even making you feel contempt. Forgive me!

Forgive me. I argue, because I do not love: this is the great truth. I have never loved you. And I would not even love you if I stayed here, even under the daily fascination of your splendid person; no: for some months I would enjoy that pleasing aesthetic-sentimental vanity which comes from having at one's side a desired and elegant woman. Nothing more. Already on other occasions I have admitted to you my great distress: no woman has ever made me suffer; I have never loved; with all of them I have only had the eagerness of desire, to begin with, and a deadly melancholy, afterwards...

Now with you, who are the most elect feminine spirit whom I have ever met, and with you who say that you love me, I have always been and wish to go on being frank: I do not love you. And the most honest decision on my part is that we should separate. I would go even if I did not have to go. However, Destiny is propitious: it imposes exile on me for other reasons too which I seize on as a pretext.

See each other again? for what purpose? One more conversation would add nothing to (or would perhaps subtract from) the fraternal good will which we ought to have for each other.

Goodbye, my good friend!

20
To Amalia Guglielminetti
Agliè Canavese, 17 April 1908

* * * In the square of my window can be seen the same landscape which I described to you this last autumn: but so different!

I regret the purple and gold of those days, nor is there any recompense to me for its loss in the tender green diffused here and there by small white and pink clouds: a landscape...such as one finds in Pastonchi, and which does not do anything for me.

The stubborn limetree which I praised to you this last autumn – you remember – is still there, but it has been cleaned up and beheaded of all its branches: and it looks comical and wretched...

The sky is grey, always full of drizzle. I am rather sad, rather bitter, but not because of this. I am sad because of the necessary separation (which does however give my soul a sense of wholesome liberation) and I am bitter because of my utter lyrical sterility.

Yesterday, the day before yesterday, I was hours and hours at my desk, piling up rhymes and thoughts and not producing one passable line... And there are so many notions, far from worthless ones, which I might develop: but I have a distressing lack of metrical will-power. I shall try again and see... * * *

21
To Marino Moretti

Turin, 29 April 1908

Alas, your postcard of this morning represents once more, and who knows till when, my renunciation of the pleasure of making your acquaintance. I am leaving this very evening for the Canavese, with my sister, who has been insisting for some days that I should leave the city. For some days I have hardly been well, Marino, or rather I have been ill: a cough, fever, a very bad mood; while I am writing to you two grams of phenacetin taken at once are roaring in my ears. It is better, much better perhaps, that you have not known me in this unhappy period; I would have turned out to be hardly congenial to you, and nothing would have upset me more.

I must leave you, because I can scarcely connect my thoughts any more. I shall write to you soon, at length, about our art as well which for some days has seemed so distant from me.

22
To Amalia Guglielminetti

Turin, 30 April 1908

Amalia, it is to you I am devoting these first lines after several days of feverish seclusion: I have hardly been well and I am in a deplorable mood. I have thought little about you during this time, and that is fortunate, because otherwise my thoughts would have been unfair to you... That is how it is: your image, like all beautiful things, only manages to get a hold on my spirit when that is serene and good and favourable.

Instead, for some days I have been sour and bad. Because so many things of ordinary life, large and small, are a torment to my sensibility and completely disastrous to my lyrical feeling.

For this reason you and your poetry have been estranged from my soul: and it makes me very sad!

Tomorrow I am definitely going back to Agliè. I hope, in the peace of the Canavese, to find my health and myself again. And I shall write to you. * * *

23
To Amalia Guglielminetti
Agliè Canavese, 24 May 1908

The other day, tearing open the envelope, I knew for certain what your letter would contain. And I read it without surprise and without grief. No, my Amalia, I shall do nothing that would make you "take up again what once impassioned you so much". The time for friendship has arrived. And it is a good thing that it has arrived. I feel, because of this, a new serenity in my soul, and the memory of our past is without regrets, very faintly suffused with just the slightest melancholy. I am writing to you from my usual room, in front of the usual window, in the very same place... The windows are closed because of the terrible wind: outside the plants are writhing and shivering in a way that is upsetting... And my soul is so quiet and so silent! It makes a strange contrast: the landscape outside and my interior landscape...

But let us talk of you, my friend; I certainly always have the right to. Of you I have lost the part which is least precious to my spirit: the loving creature, but I still have the other part, the only part for which I truly care: the good friend, the companion who is *necessary*. * * *

24
To Amalia Guglielminetti
Ronco Canavese, 20 June 1908

* * * I was to have sailed on the 25th of this month for America! And almost without touching land I would have gone, by way of Tierra del Fuego, Japan, India, etc... *Around the world*, but not in 80 days as in my youth...

They have *promised* me that after about two years of *uninterrupted* life at sea I shall return home permanently healthy and strong. As I say, I was about to leave on the 25th. Then the season was judged to be unfavourable and I shall sail, instead, this coming November. As you might have known, it is a novelty which frightens me, but does not charm me, and I am undertaking it more because I am tempted by the physical benefit than out of artistic curiosity... There is no art, in my opinion, outside Italy, and the whole world must be uniform like the novels of Pierre Loti. So it seems to me.

There is no news at present. I am writing some few things and at certain times I am not dissatisfied with myself. At certain other times, however, I am so demoralised that I should like to die. The things I have sketched out, the verses polished with great labour seem to me to be contemptible efforts and I should like to give them all to the flames and recover permanently from the Tuberculosis of literature.

But since I know I shall never recover, I brighten up, take up my poor papers again, and resignedly continue with my useless work.

This is a comfort: having already in front of me the whole plan of the future volume, and cherishing it in my imagination as it will be when completed. It will be organic and cyclical, although made up of so many separate pieces, almost all rather long narrative poems. * * *

25
To Amalia Guglielminetti
Ronco Canavese, 3 August 1908

How gloomy it is today! I am writing to you just to comfort myself a little. The valley is all misty, the sky an apocalyptic grey. And I am alone! * * *

My life goes on here monotonously and healthily, as I like it. But my leisure is not inactive: I study a great deal every day:

I want to graduate in autumn, before my exile. I do not want to cross the Ocean except as a Doctor of Laws. * * *

I could bundle my things together, complete those I have started, revise those that are rough, but it would take some months, several months. And from today until the end of November I shall be caught up in the pettifogging legal whirlwind. But now, wait: I am writing without thinking, as is my habit.

There is some question of a new edition of the *Way of Refuge* with an unpublished section added? I certainly could do this, adding Signorina Domestica and some other narrative poems, but in this way I would remove the principal groundwork for that other future volume, which is very precious to me. And might it not be a *rehash* which could jeopardise my spotless literary record? Would this *hotchpotch* be pleasing? Might it not be a fruit gathered before time? By waiting another year I could send to press a whole volume of unpublished pieces: so would it not be a better course of action to wait? * * *

26
To Amalia Guglielminetti
Ronco Canavese, 3 September 1908

How my studies weigh upon me! I have just left my course-sheets (oh so many! Heaps of 1000-1500 pages!) on a chair, on the balcony, held down by a stone, so that the wind will not take them with it into the valley. And I have salved my conscience with the pretext of writing to you, although I have not really anything to say to you...

So we shall be together for a while. Today is a day when I love you. I returned from Ivrea yesterday evening after being away three days. I had been made very tired by very serious things: and I had had to be active, decisive, outspoken, farsighted, penetrating, and vulgar.

Just imagine me!

But I have a taste for venturing upon things which smack of qualities I do not possess.

Today I am exhausted, but very pleased with myself.

At Ivrea, on the reading-desk in the hotel, I browsed through an ancient number of *La Donna* and I read one of your poems: I was lost. Then I went out into the sunny afternoon, and I went wandering through the gardens by the side of the Dora and along the sad provincial roads, thinking of you at some length, as has not happened to me for a long time.

I like Ivrea. It is a little copperplate engraving of a town, with its towers, its small deserted squares, its shops selling old-fashioned knick-knacks... It is a suitable destination for one-day breaks, for overnight stays. Because of this, in front of the unsophisticated shop-windows or in the old grassy arcades, I thought about you a great deal. And I was anxious about you, feeling a very keen longing for you. And so I drifted, lost: arousing the curiosity of those good inhabitants who were surviving in the summer heat. Then – my errands were finished – I left Ivrea for Cuorgné, then left Cuorgné for Pont, by train, then left Pont for Ronco by cab. A long and varied journey, tiring, not sad: and at night I came back into the little house which you have visited and sat down to supper, alone, in the yellow light of a homely lamp. I am alone, for my Mother, my brother, all of them have gone away: and I shall stay here, alone, until almost the end of September. Coming back into this house yesterday evening, I was ashamed of how I had thought about you some hours before, in the deserted little town. Here, in this very poor and peaceful house, a pure boyish soul comes to meet me, after every absence, as soon as I have crossed the threshold: it drives out from my spirit everything which is not good. And it is with this soul that I am writing to you today. * * *

For quite a time I have not thought about my literary dreams, I alternate study and entomological interests: I am breeding an extraordinary colony of caterpillars. I want to get from them some observations and many beautiful photographs to illustrate a book of natural history which I have dreamed of for some time: *Butterflies*.

I shall see to it after the volume of verse: but I am beginning to collect material for the text and for the illustrations. You will see what a novel and beautiful thing it is. Just picture to yourself that in a case I have about three hundred chrysalids of all species, obtained from caterpillars bred with infinite patience, for weeks and weeks; now they are almost all suspended from the grating of the lid and have taken the strange shape of stylised crustaceans for a lady's necklace.

In a few days they will be butterflies. In fact, I want to send you some chrysalids: do not laugh, I beg you. I am attracted by the thought that they will open up in your room, among your ribbons and your perfumes. Extract them from the box in which I shall dispatch them to you, WITHOUT TOUCHING THEM, *lifting* FROM THE SIDES *the* COTTON *where they are laid* and put them without displacing them from the bed of cotton *into a bigger container, where the future butterfly will have enough room to spread its wings.* And leave them in peace, like sleeping infants: *without touching them, or disturbing them*: in a fortnight they will be born.

You will write to me and describe their colours; and from the other side of Piedmont you will tell me what has been said to you on my behalf by the beautiful prisoners, who fell asleep in this valley and have reawakened on the hills of a distant region...

And do not smile too much at these things, more beautiful and more profound than many others in their power to console our melancholy... * * *

27
To Amalia Guglielminetti
Ronco Canavese, 17 September 1908

My chrysalids are all butterflies!

I discovered it today, through the mesh of the lid: I closed the windows and opened the box and there was, in my big bright room, a stormy rustling of disconcerted prisoners.

There are a hundred, more than a hundred: and all of the genus Vanessa: Vanessa Atalanta and Vanessa Io.

I am sending both kinds to you; ponder on their beauty: the one is made of live coals and of shadows like certain of your sonnets, the other has the look of anger or of anguish.

And with them I am enclosing for you the two empty shells, wretched as barren beanpods, so that you may reflect on the marvel, my Friend...

And do not smile at your fanatical companion: I want to introduce you to these things; and this I shall do in the book I have mentioned: a volume of letters: letters to you, rather archaic like those which abbots used to write to eighteenth-century gentlewomen to introduce them to the mysteries of Physics, of Astronomy, of Mechanics; but very modern in content, made up of new philosophical observations and curious boyish fancies. You will see.

This, like my other dearest aims, is very uncertain and distant. But I shall write this book, *I swear to you.*

For the present I am, at intervals, attending to Signorina Domestica: the first half is almost completed; it needs one canto and some stanzas here and there... Will it be good? Will it be liked? Sometimes I like it and sometimes not. Certainly it took a great deal of perseverance: and that, unfortunately, is not apparent from the style, which is deliberately low (although it is in triple rhyme)... But I shall not publish it by itself: *I shall lighten it* with a fragmentary and exotic intermezzo, and perhaps with a prelude (started off by *The Colloquies*) and with an epilogue: so the volume will be varied and cyclical at the same time...

And all this will take at least a year and a half.

Today I am talking about myself too much: it is for me a day of anxious hope: I do not know...

Perhaps I have caught it from the new-born infants: I believe that such is the state of mind of butterflies when, still swaddled in the chrysalis, they sense that the time for flying is imminent...

Many have not come out, however: they have turned dark, turbid, dry: they are dead: and yet they too cherished their illusions for so long...

And yours, your chrysalids? What are they doing, beautiful foster-mother? Send me news of them and of yourself. * * *

28
To Giulio De Frenzi
Agliè Canavese, 6 October 1908

Yes, yes, I have received your beautiful sad letter: thank you. And pardon the silence: I did not reply to you out of fear, I swear, of boring you.

Like all exiles I do not know what to talk about if I do not talk about myself: and for this reason I write little and not very willingly. For some time, then, I have been going through a grey phase of perplexities of anxieties of extravagant distress, and I cannot help noticing, once again, my distressing unfitness for practical life. I have not even written much verse. But I have daydreamed and meditated a great deal. And I have conceived and constructed the outline of my future volume: an idyll in two sections and an intermezzo, a kind of narrative poem composed of various short poems, joined to each other by a cyclical link: a difficult and very precise thing in its style although romantic light and innocent in content. I could send you some fragments (part of the first section) but I absolutely refuse to do so; there is in the trepidation of the poet in front of the good judge a little of the flirtatiousness of a beautiful woman (or one who thinks herself such): she does not wish to present herself for judgement without the final ribbon and final touch of powder.

I have had, recently, a long struggle between my vanity and my good sense: Guido Treves, unasked, has of his own free will offered me the hospitality of the "bijou" series; Dino Mantovani wrote to me of this after he had met Treves at Lago Maggiore, and he advised me to republish the *Way of Refuge* together with a new section. And the new section does not exist! (The idyll of which I have spoken to you will only be publishable after a year, perhaps more.) I could add some insignificant poems (*The colloquies, Cocotte,* etc.) but I am afraid that this rehash (and in a kitchen as noisy as that of Treves) would not gain for me any new fraternal spirits and would alienate the old ones from me a little. *You* tell me, with your fine literary tact, is not this a false step which is proposed to me? It would be immediate, for December: a thing so precipitate that it would be contrary to the calmness of my usual method. I have replied to Mantovani in the negative: have I made a mistake?

At any rate I would not see the volume. At the end of November I shall already be far away in barbarous lands from where I shall think of literature as of those pictures which, as children, we used to put together again from jumbled blocks. Oh well!...

In a few days I am returning to Turin for many examinations and for a very unlikely degree; then I shall be in Genoa for some weeks, then I do not know where: "in any country whatsoever, so long as it is out of this world" and out of the civilised world especially, a country without a past, where they do not talk of the Latin Renaissance, of Nietzsche, of d'Annunzio, of Energy and of Buddha: therefore not the East not Greece not Egypt etc... It is a mirage which comforts me because I have seen very little of the world and the idea of a long sea-voyage makes me feel giddy. * * *

29
To Amalia Guglielminetti
Agliè Canavese, 14 October 1908

I have been to Turin again, swept along in a whirlwind of wearying affairs; I shall be there again shortly, for my examinations which I detest. When my university time has elapsed (two weeks, not less) I shall allow myself the reward of visiting you.

I shall bring to you, probably, only half of my person and of my soul, I shall be so tired and empty and impaired... I too desire very much to see you again although it seems to me that I have not anything to say to you. They will be my last days in Italy and we want to take away a sensible memory of each other.

You are my dearest Friend, dear Amalia: the others, some more some less, have all disappointed me.

124

30
To Amalia Guglielminetti

Genoa, 10 December 1908

I have just come back from saying goodbye to a visitor. It is seven in the evening; it is nighttime already; outside the sea is howling, a dreadful sea and sky.

Here I am where and how I wanted to be, but I have still not found myself again. I am looking for myself and not finding myself. Because of this I am rather sad: I have in myself that unease which you certainly will recognise – that being without ourselves –. Having had, that is, your future purpose eclipsed for days, the thread of your dream and thought broken. But it will pass – I know myself well – it will pass very soon, and then I shall have a reaction of serene energy. My life here is such as you know. I have found again the same places the same sea the same people; and the same spacious solitude which has become by now so necessary to me… Everything should be favourable to work; and instead this sea induces the most sluggish idleness, it persuades to a contemplative dreaming, without words. And my active anxiety suffers a great deal from it.

There is only one thing which I look after diligently: my health. Every day I have two injections of two doses each; and I am so saturated with resinous essences, with camphor, with creosote, that the aromatic savour spreads from the blood into the palate: something that is incompatible with the taste of a fruit or a beef-steak… * * *

31
To Amalia Guglielminetti

Turin, 1 February 1909

Thank you for your kind words.

Poor Amalia, how are you managing these days?

For a month (I was summoned here by a telegram on the second of January) I have been a nurse, among doctors and sisters, without an hour of respite, with scarcely a moment free for meals and necessary rest.

I have spent some terrible days.

Now my Mother's life is safe, but this longed-for and unexpected joy does not suffice to calm me completely.

For months I have had in the depths of my soul something sad and inconsolable which I do not understand. For a long time

I have not understood myself any more. Oh well!...

And your sister?

I beg you to send news of her, and I reciprocate for her the good wishes that you sent for my Mother.

And your dreams? And our dreams? Oh well!... The last voice of selfishness in these days of complete self-renunciation is the voice of my poetry. And for months and months I shall have to keep even this one good thing quiet. This is all I complain about.

Tell me how your sister is: I shall give you further news of my patient, and let us encourage each other, my Amalia, and love each other.

32
To Marino Moretti
Turin, 11 February 1909

I should be in Tenerife, in the shade of the palmtrees, and instead I am here, summoned by a telegram to come to my mother who has been very gravely ill and whose condition is still grave. A stroke has injured her permanently, reducing her to a shadow of the fine svelte young woman she was before. I am here, as I say, I do not know how...

In my complete self-renunciation the voice of art, which I am so fond of, makes itself heard shrilly and most painfully. And who knows how long it will be before I am able to take up again the thread of my dreams! Oh well!... * * *

33
To Amalia Guglielminetti
Turin, 25 February 1909

Here I am, still here, but I do not know how... For two months now I have been leading such a life that my ego has estranged itself from it permanently and I do not know myself any longer.

That is how I am, my Amalia; when the time of affliction comes, my personality, fearful of suffering, goes away I do not know where, and another personality comes in its place, which I do not like.

I do not really like myself any more; and not even you would like me, even though you are so tolerant.

But let us talk of our invalids: how is your sister?

My Mother is now out of danger.

126

But the life she still has is such that I, supporting her under the arms to make her try out her first steps and contemplating in silence that face which is not (and will not ever again be) hers, feel a *deadly* pity enter into me, an unmentionable regret... And just imagine what my inner life is like these days!

Not to mention the practical side of my life: I am downright degraded! For some time I have been almost completely unable to sleep, overwhelmed continuously by a thousand duties: not the least the financial administration, conversations with rough men, notaries, lawyers, tenants, farmers... Oh well! I cannot manage any more of it! The last survivor of myself is my poetry: how tenacious one's ego is of the art which it likes! Is it not like this with you too? * * *

34
To Giulio De Frenzi

Turin, 5 March 1909

You will have received my last letter, which was not a very happy one. Pardon me. The not so sad thing which I have to tell you is this. One of my poems will figure in the *Nuova Antologia* for the middle of March, an idyll which I lived two summers ago and which I resuscitated in rhyme last summer, with love and with great labour. I have already corrected and returned the first proofs. Would you mind, dear De Frenzi, obliging me with the names of some genuine connoisseurs for the customary homage; and not so much in the hope of critical complicity (very welcome!) as for some likely friendships. I am very ingenuous and very unsociable, a novice in the literary world which I hate rather. Help me then with some names. * * *

35
To Amalia Guglielminetti

Turin, 11 March 1909

After my first fraternal words at that dreadful time I did not wish to write to you again until you had wept all your tears. But today I received your letter and met Erminia... So I am writing to you, but without knowing what to say and how to say it... Poor Amalia!

Consider that I am writing to you from the bedside of my Mother, who is permanently impaired: at hand I have Sister Giulia of the

Nazarenes, who has been watching by her for three months. From Sister Giulia (who had it from Sister Gaudenzia) I used to get news every day, I used to follow step by step the way of Sorrow in your home...

And one evening I gathered, from the Sister's silent signs, across my Mother's bed, that news which is without remedy! My Mother understood immediately and burst out sobbing and we wept the whole evening – *I swear this to you* on her recovery! –

We wept all evening as for a daughter and a sister – Amalia, my poor good companion, here we are in front of Grief, that thing of which our youth has always been ignorant up to now.

Let us pluck up courage: and I more than you! Time will soothe every wound, for you. For me it will not. You will be able to resuscitate with the magic art of poetry her whom you no longer have. I shall not be able to. I shall have for years and years, in front of me, in my home, the mere shadow of her who was my young and svelte Mother... Consider which of the two disasters is the more terrible!

You have another comfort: you can sing your grief. I know that you have composed something very charming for the departed soul. I do not have this advantage. My poetry does not console me in grief: I am afraid of suffering; poetry does not accompany me, and I do not beguile it with beautiful dreams in my pleasant leisure. * * *

36
To Giulio De Frenzi

Turin, 1 May 1909

Either my idyll failed to please you (and I should be sorry for that!) and you are so good as to remain silent about it to me, or your letter has gone astray, or you are somewhat harassed by your responsibility for the printing of the *Antologia*, or... I do not know! I suffer from your silence (not for your complicity as a critic which I shall have need of in a few years), but because you are one of the ten spirits for whom I publish my verse. And for one line from you I would give the whole heap of fraternal letters which I have received from fine Italian names.

I shall leave Turin within days. My Mother is permanently ill, I am permanently not very well, life is rubbish, there is no good except the art which gives us pleasure.

Write and comfort me.

37
To Marino Moretti

Turin, 3 May 1909

Pardon me, pardon me: I am unpardonable; but if you knew, if you saw what a fearful life, what a continual renunciation has been mine for some months! My mother is as usual; that is, she is ill; and on me, who am absolutely incapable, presses all the burden of primogeniture. I do not have one moment of peaceful resignation, but, although I do not fall short of my duty, I thrash about like a boy who has been put in the corner. And I do not see, for the present, any liberation: except one: a terrible one.

In my mission as a nurse I console myself with our art: but even poetry has been bitter to me for some time: it follows me only through periods of pleasant leisure and abandons me when the time for suffering and the need for consolation have come.

38
To Amalia Guglielminetti

Bertesseno Viù, 15 June 1909

* * * You who study and sing the subtleties of the soul, explain this strange enigma to me... – Dear Amalia, I am rather sad. And so tired. And so dreadfully alone! This hermitage is two hours from Turin by train, almost three by stage-coach, more than two by mule, and almost one on foot, among crags and boulders of a Dantesque ruggedness.

The place is beautiful, but my shelter is so mystic and so dreary that the hovel at Ronco seems a palace in comparison. All the same I resign myself with a smile, through that taste which you know is in me for humble things: a kind of dilettantish literary humility... Not to mention that I could not find anywhere better for my physical peace and for my interior life which has been darkened for so many months... – What silence, my Amalia! I am writing to you on a little rustic balcony with in front of me a bunch of large buttercups which have just been gathered and are standing in a kitchen-tumbler. Beyond the wooden railing the emerald emptiness of the valley drops away... It is beautiful. But I cannot stop myself being rather sad. * * *

39
To Giulio De Frenzi

Bertesseno Viù, 15 June 1909

Thank you for your thanks: they have reached me in this alpine retreat where I am staying in order to recover from the six terrible months spent at the bedside of my mother (who is a little better) and where I am trying to take up again the thread of my dreams. But I am so tired, so impaired, so debased... I am collecting butterflies. I am considering a volume on these creatures. I am a deeply serious and passionately keen entomologist and I should like to transfuse into a series of letters to a lady all the poetry which emanates from lepidoptera. I shall have to become a ten year old child once more in order to see these things again with worthy eyes... I shall try. Dear De Frenzi, remember me. And when you remember me, send me simply a newspaper together with your pieces, if possible. Here the world's news is almost interesting.

40
To Amalia Guglielminetti

Bertesseno Viù, 13 July 1909

I have been waiting for a happy hour to write to you: and one has come today, with the latest number of *Donna*, thanks to Giulia Cavallari-Cantalamessa (there is something of her even in the name...).
Ah!... But who is this woman?
    ... *At Italy's and at Savoy's sweet cry all things are rising...*
Have you read it? You should read it again...
I am rolling about on my deck-chair, and I am weeping with laughter, calling upon the pindaric singer to come into my arms...
Poor Amalia! With regard to art, there are among you ladies bunglers more atrocious almost than among us men...
Enough of this. Do you know that I have left my retreat for a week and have strolled idly down into the valley as far as Balme? Perhaps I shall move my tents into some region of the valley; because, having clambered up into this solitude, I feel myself too fearfully dead to human society. * * *
I have read, with involuntary satisfaction, the fine demolition job which has been done on Teresa. Good old Borgese! That volume (you did not say so out of caution and because of the circumstances...) is solemn trash.

And that distinguished young lady is a worthy friend of Marinetti's...

This is a rabble, both male and female, towards whom I am implacable. Malefactors who in two months spin out a volume of 300 pages and have the presumption to get themselves called poets!

Ah! The slow and patient work, the renunciation and the concentration directed to this one end, the scrupulous *labor limae* which alone results in beautiful and lasting work... But these people are just greedy adventurers. * * *

41
To Amalia Guglielminetti
Bertesseno Viù, 25 September 1909

Why has there been silence between us for so long? And yet I remember you, one could say, at every hour, and I feel that you remember me at least three times a week... Do I deceive myself?

I came back up here again two days ago, after some wandering about: one stay of a couple of weeks in Viù itself (for some gaiety...) one trip to Turin (for some melancholy) two to Genoa (for some bitter-sweetness) and several to my Mother: for something very sad: her health which is always always always distressing...

You cannot, or perhaps you can, imagine what a perpetual shadow envelops my youth on this account.

Think of the dreadful days which preceded the release of your poor Emma, think of them prolonged for months, for years, in an agony with no way out! * * *

42
To his sister Erina
Aosta, 30 July 1910

The news is still very good. I have got my appetite back and I eat a lot of butter and drink excellent milk. The air suits me and is not causing me any of the troubles threatened by the doctors.

Tomorrow my friends are leaving and only I shall stay here with a Genoese family who are stopping until autumn. I want to vegetate for twenty days so that I may feel completely recovered. Write.

I spend a large part of the day on the long terrace which you can see on this postcard. It is a real sanatorium.

43
To the editor of *Il Momento*
Agliè Canavese, 22 October 1910

Your kind request comes to me in this retreat in the Canavese where I am correcting the proofs of the volume of verse which the house of Treves will bring out in December: *The Colloquies*. The collection will bring together the least unsuccessful of my published and unpublished lyrics and will be a kind of synthesis of my first youth, a pale reflection of my inner drama.

The poems – although independent – will be united by a fine cyclical thread and divided into three parts:

I – The youthful error: episodes of sentimental vagrancy;

II – On the threshold: adumbrating some colloquies with death;

III – The Veteran: "to him, the veteran of Love and Death, they lied to him, those two fine things..." and it will reflect the mind of one who, having surmounted every physical and moral calamity, resigns himself to life with a smile.

What literary and artistic objects have I pursued? I do not know.

I do not believe that the artist, and the poet in particular, can or should be conscious of his feelings, clearsighted with regard to his art and his aim. And I believe next that it is a dangerous and difficult thing to speak of them publicly. The poems which I am assembling are not my work, but the work of my life, of my adolescence and of my youth; it is I who have made the verses – to the best of my ability; now that I am assembling them I can perhaps observe in them as a whole a tendency which rewards me for my labours and comforts me: an ascent from sensual and morbid sadness to the most serene idealism.

Today I believe in the spirit; I feel, I know in myself the life of the spirit. From that too well received *Way of Refuge*, sinning here and there in its ingenuous materialism, my faith has been raised in these *Colloquies* to purer and more consolatory speculations. I do not know if this is my road to Damascus, nor if I shall move in the future to a dogmatic faith, but I feel that this is the way of salvation.

I hope I may be allowed to pass over the third and fourth questions of your courteous inquiry in silence. I read almost no novels or short stories, I do not bother with the theatre, and in my fields of interest – poetry, philosophy, natural sciences – I am not able to and I do not wish to make my mark.

I do not really understand the meaning of nationalist literature, of idealist literature, but I believe firmly in the genius of Italy and in the ideal. How can an Italian not be Italian? And how can a masterpiece not be a work of pure idealism?

The very phase of positivism which we have been through teaches us that positivism was an illusion, that the apologias for matter and for "mad brutishness" were empty. Nietzsche himself, Schopenhauer himself – I cite two of the most glorious publicists of matter and instinct – did not realise that, in denying it, they were exalting the spirit. Idealism starts up from the very song of him who denies it, and he who denies it is like one who is singing and who stops his ears so as not to hear his own voice. But today no one denies the spirit any more. Empty words – today – are Darwinism, materialism, positivism.

And so there is a trembling new idealism, a need for faith. Even the religious crisis, and the heresies which trouble the Church, are evidence that spiritual problems are being discussed by those uncertain spirits who at one time ranged themselves with atheists and with those who are indifferent. The word "soul" no longer makes intellectuals smile, as it did scarcely twenty years ago, but it makes them curious and thoughtful.

My last point: the necessity of Christian moralisation. I believe firmly in this too, but I cannot separate morality and Christianity. True morality cannot fail to coincide at all points with the teaching of Christ. * * *

44
To Marino Moretti

Turin, 9 March 1911

I am grateful to you for the kind remembrance and for the kind words. And the first copy of *The Colloquies* which I am able to get will be for you. You are one of the twelve fraternal spirits for whom I publish my daydreams.

I have seen Teresa – for a brief half-hour and in a circle of friends which cut me off from her – but I was enraptured with her; she is a delightful fragile creature, beyond my expectation in every way. And she will bring my greetings to you in return.

If you are not happy, be comforted. For many months I too have been going through dark days, and neither the good offices of friends nor my literary vanities have been able to cheer me up. But my troubles are of a very real family kind: business affairs, bonds, duties, relatives, law-suits. And I used to hope for so little from life. * * *

45

To his sister Erina and her
mother-in-law Mamma Giordano

Naples – (in an hour
we are going on land
to send telegrams and
letters). *S.S. Raffaele
Rubattino.*
18 February 1912

I wish I could write you a proper letter; you will get instead
just a few rambling lines simply because my head is spinning
(not through sea-sickness which we have not suffered from at
all) but because we have just got up from the table and we drink
dry Capri with our meals, so that everyone is in a state of semi-
intoxication. But health and morale are both excellent. The two
nights on board I have slept very well; nothing disagreeable has
happened either to me or to Garrone. The sea and sky are marvel-
lous, the catering is beyond all our hopes: a real exhibition of
gastronomy where my appetite, for the moment, cuts a poor
figure. Even Garrone is sorry that he cannot gobble up every-
thing. We have been introduced to the Captain who received us
most cordially and already knew my name and was as courteous
to us as the others were. We are seated by him at table and are
already well acquainted with him. By now we no longer feel
ourselves *alone in the world* but protected and at peace in every
way. So do not be fearful about anything. There have not been
any disagreeable episodes, however slight. * * *

And now, how can we thank you and Mamma Giordano for
your *tour de force* the other day? Even I, who know you, was
amazed by it, and your efficiency and Mamma's astounded the
good Garrone who sends grateful thanks... I was happy because
you changed a day's drudgery into an almost pleasant day,
despite the sad hour of separation... To me it seems like a dream
and indeed I cannot describe to you the indefinable effect which
it made on me. Perhaps an effect analogous to that which it made
on you.

I am unpacking the trunks and suitcases and at Port Said I shall
separate the stuff to leave out and put it on one side, trying (but
in vain!) to imitate Mamma Giordano's efficiency... Everything
is so well arranged that one would think it was set in order by a

conjurer! Thank her for this and for everything, for the demonstration of affection which she chose to give me, putting herself out as far as Genoa for me.

I think you have the list of the ports, but always put (as well as the city) *Raffaele Rubattino, Maritime Services*. After the dates of the ports have expired, our address will be: National Society Agency – Maritime Services – P.O. Box 142 – Bombay (India). * * *

46
To his sister Erina
Red Sea, 28 February 1912

Here we are at the end of this very long sea; the passage (which has lasted almost eight days from Suez) was longer than that famous one of the Hebrews, but I think it was more amusing: we have experienced all the most pleasing emotions, from that biblical one of Mount Sinai where we passed very close, to that patriotic one of Massawa where we were stopped by the Italian fleet with two torpedo-boats: the *Granatiere* and the *Garibaldino* escorted us the whole day to protect us from the Arabian Turks.

This evening at ten o'clock we arrive at Aden where I shall post this letter of mine and hope to find news of you. Our news could not be better. Health more than satisfactory, not a hint of sea-sickness, not the slightest upset.

I have become accustomed to the English bill of fare, which is no small thing! And truly this ordered life on board ship is ideal to restore one's health: I think we shall leave the ship with real regret. By now we are quite at home and the best of friends with everyone. The heat and the light are of an intensity of which one can have no notion, even in the month of August: and yet we are not in the least uncomfortable; perhaps because the sea air alleviates the stuffiness.

It is a time of triumph for skinny people, because anyone who is at all florid is reduced to complete inertia and perpetual perspiration... We all dress in white, with no cardigans allowed; in the evening, however, it takes us half an hour to get ready and put on our dinner-jackets: it is the invariable custom, and will be even in India, so they tell me: the day is spent in one's shirt and the evening in formal clothes... * * * There is a fair number of us travellers: several ladies, but all elderly; almost all English people who are returning to India after travelling in Europe: a strange society which I shall describe to you when we meet. * * *

47
To his mother
Colombo, 9 April 1912

We are on a trip to Colombo, the capital, to arrange for our departure. We have bought tickets for Bombay, from where we should depart the 15th or the 25th of April, so that by the beginning of May or on the 15th of May I should be home. And we shall embrace each other again *certainly* before your anniversary. My health continues to be good, Ceylon is a paradise which never wearies me, but I am aware that I have duties at home and I do not want to prolong your anxious expectation any further. I hope that you have received my letters more regularly than I have been receiving yours. I am sure that you write to me often and at length, but the fact that the letters come via Bombay means that they are diverted and delayed dreadfully. When we call in at Bombay and other ports I shall collect the post that has been delayed. Meanwhile you would be wise to address your letters to Catania, in Sicily, because they would not find us here any more.

I shall arrive in time to start exploring the countryside round Agliè with you, and I confess to you that after the beauty of the too huge and monstrous vegetation of Ceylon I think almost with relief of the gentle and restful green of the Canavese. I hope that we may spend a summer there that is quiet and even serene. You will see!

Meanwhile be brave during these few weeks that we are still separated, and think that every hour brings us many kilometres closer. To while away the time of waiting, follow the boat's course on the map; I shall do the same. * * *

48
To Marino Moretti
Turin, 13 January 1914

Here, for the *Illustrazione*, is an extract from the *Butterflies*, the first bit of my virginal manuscript to see the light.

The poem will be published in spring with illustrations by me which I am now completing. It has an air of the eighteenth-century didactic poets: Mascheroni and Rucellai, but I have tried to remove the academic starch and the archaic dust in order to transfuse our restless modern spirit into it, while still respecting the models and their ritual. So the poem is dedicated to one Alba

Nigra – a fabled Lesbia Cidonia of our days – and is divided into two books, composed of eighteen epistles. In the first book I follow the metamorphosis of a family of Vanessa Io butterflies: egg caterpillar chrysalid butterfly, until I open the window of my room to the "flying multitude" of the prisoners. In the second book I consider in fourteen scientific-sentimental monographs the different species of butterflies, domestic and foreign. The poem will be published simultaneously in German, translated by Signora Elena Brank Franchi, the wife of the famous Berlin painter.

Those are some things to say, if you think a couple of covering words would be opportune. Do you think the illustrations are necessary? I am afraid of making some scientific errors (the caterpillars and the chrysalids which are spoken about are of the genus Vanessa, not easy to find and to represent faithfully and artistically). I would prefer any kind of allegorical fantasy or independent ornamental design. Or even nothing. I await your reply.

49
To Mamma Giordano
Agliè Canavese, 19 August 1915

I regret that my health, which is still indifferent, prevents me from making a trip to Feletto. I am following Gramegna's cure of almost complete rest. Every day I take a little walk to the foot of the hill and rest for long hours under the chestnuts. This physical and moral laziness seems to help me very much, in fact I am beginning to eat with less reluctance. My condition has not worsened; it is just that I feel sometimes a slight palpitation of the heart. But I hope it will pass, because I have suffered from it before. * * *

50
To his godmother Adele Testa-Tapparo
Sturla, 25 June 1916

I would not have dared to write to you directly, and I am grateful to you for having broken the silence between us, all the more grateful because I had the same thing in mind as you: to sketch the image of poor Ugo in some truly heartfelt pages. But to do this worthily we must avoid all celebratory rhetoric and all platitudes, we must shun academic eulogy and the clichés which today are so profanely abused for all of the fallen.

Those pages must not be suitable for anyone at all but him.

We shall, my dear Godmother, be able to initiate a beautiful and distressing piece of work: so distressing as to become almost a comfort; trying to revive his image through your grief as a mother and mine as a friend. But I would need to have, as my intimate and assiduous collaborator, your inexpressible distress. Are you up to that? Do you wish to start now?

You are surrounded by devoted relatives; you can dictate. Dictate, without any hesitation as to the way of going about it and without any literary preoccupations, everything that flashes across your poor tormented mind. I, for my part, shall try to reply to you as well as I can; I shall not try to relieve, but to encourage your grief, mitigating it; at times I shall be able to do that.

Certain incurable wounds have to be reopened every day, they need the daily application of a red-hot iron; yours is one of those griefs which have to be exacerbated every day in order to gain relief; your grief does not wish for oblivion, it would be offensive and irreverent if I proposed it to you. Let us not forget then, but remember, remember to the point of agony.

To revive one who is no more.

It is not difficult. Notice that it is easier to live with the dead than with the living. Have you ever observed that, when we see again a loved one who has been absent, after half an hour we no longer have anything to talk about, and there comes an embarrassing silence or an empty conversation? With the living we have only speech, with the dead we have that spiritual communion which is worth any kind of living together.

I know that the loss of poor Ugo has struck home more than a thousand other such cases; you are more unhappy than innumerable other mothers who weep the same tears as you; but I am looking for, and I seem to find, some subtle considerations to comfort myself and to comfort you. Yes, fate has cut short one of the most fortunate lives I have ever known; youth, health, good looks (he had his own distinct kind of nordic beauty, which had even increased with the years), a lively mind, a happily adaptable serenity, the adoration of his loved ones, the easy circumstances of a gentleman: in short, all the qualities which cause a young man to be described as "enviable". But do you think that destiny would have been so kind as to preserve these qualities in him through other vicissitudes, through another forty years? You will say to me that your cup was already brimful, that in the tragic gloom of blindness which surrounds you your misfortune is more hopeless than that of any other mother... Perhaps it is not so; perhaps you are losing him a little less, because you had already resigned yourself to having lost him a little; you were already accustomed to relinquishing him, to relinquishing "that which is seen", and to communicating with him as with a spirit: is not the spirit something which you perceive today just as you used to? I shall explain to you later when we meet how from the paganistic materialism of one time I have evolved to an almost religiously spiritual position: providential for one who cannot find comfort in the dogmas of a traditional faith. And I shall read to you a few pages from philosophical and Buddhist texts, the only books which can still interest a despairing spirit like yours, to which – I suppose – what happens and what will happen on this earth is a matter of indifference, by now…

Everything is a matter of indifference, except the image of the absent loved one: and we shall be able to revive this image unimpaired, with a correspondence starting now; or with our conversations at Agliè, very soon…

I need your memories. Mine are those of a friend, a most affectionate friend, but they do not suffice.

It is strange that there should flash across my mind, today, the first and last impressions which bind me to his mortal form. I remember the first time I was permitted to see him in your home at Agliè; in the next to last room, before the terrace on the corner; I had been outside, opposite the vine which was putting forth some enormous clusters (even the tiniest details have a value in our inner world, do they not?) and in the open doorway was the outline of your mother – Granny – bent over what was obviously a cot, and around there was my father, my mother, and some other uncertain figures; my family were making some humorous remarks to you which I do not remember; they were laughing, they were delighted; I looked at your mother's hands which were handling with such ease the little body, quite white, quite bare. He had one tiny foot in his mouth and his eyes were shut tight. Then his eyes opened, first one and then the other, and I was able to see the blue of his eyes; that blue which all your family have, Peppina, Carlo, Felice, all of you. Then the little one was wrapped up in his swaddling-clothes (I think you had unwrapped him for a few minutes) and I know I had a feeling of anguish at those little legs being squeezed and imprisoned. That is the first time I saw him. The last time was twenty years later, some years ago. I had gone to Turin from Agliè, for one day, oppressed by the summer heat and engaged on the most ordinary tasks. In via Roma I felt a hand on my shoulder: it was he. Bold, young, healthy.

I had an hour available; I took his arm, I made him come with me, happy with that cheerfulness and youthfulness at my side. We went in to take an aperitif and our two figures looked as if they were in a large advertisement.

– Ugo, just think that they used to insult you by finding some resemblance between us!

– And yet you do rather call me to mind...

– Yes, as a disinterred ancestor calls to mind his twenty-year-old descendant!

I remember that he laughed a lot and did not have the courage to lie.

– Yes, I do find you rather run down; you ought to cure yourself properly...

And he spoke to me for a long time about a hypernutritional cure which he had undergone himself, at Palermo, and he took a real interest in my case. And while he was speaking I noticed once more one of his essential qualities, a quality which is very rare in young and happy people: kindness. He was kind. He had a heart which was not closed to the suffering of others. While he was speaking he fixed me with those bright eyes of his under their blond lashes, with a look of thoughtless affectionate pity which mortified me rather, but which also gave me a comforting sense of brotherhood.

He was determined to give me all the time he had at his disposal, he accompanied me everywhere, even to my tailor; he spared me the effort of speaking; he spoke for me, he chose, he frayed the material out, he felt it, he discussed, he bargained, with that easy way of speaking he had and that gentlemanly aplomb of his.

How he loved life and the things that make life beautiful!

Walking along, talking to me, he kept a lookout for anything beautiful that could be enjoyed: ladies, motor cars, knick-knacks in shop-windows, fabrics, footwear, silverware, jewels, sweets, perfumes; everything which promotes the perpetual illusion. And he spoke of them as an expert and a philosopher: a wise philosopher who knows how to desire and yet not suffer from unsatisfied desire. How happy I felt he was! It seemed that a little of that happiness communicated itself even to me; and meanwhile he was dwelling upon hypernutrition and the results which I would achieve in less than a month. Alas! He did not think that the secret of the cure was his twenty years, his good nerves, his sound health, his peaceful and serene philosophy! We parted on a tramcar...

I thought of him for a long time, almost with a feeling of envy

140

except that I loved him in the way one does love a dear brother who is ten years younger. What a pity! – I thought – The years will pass, and grief will come even for him!

And I never would have supposed that for him the years were not going to come, and not even Grief!

Death has released him from the inevitable law: this thought should mitigate your dreadful grief, my poor dear Godmother!

I wanted to tell you of these impressions of mine because they are like the first and the last page of what I know about him. Between these two I could write hundreds more, all dear to our memories; memories which sketch his image at Agliè, at Cornigliano, in Turin, at Rivarossa, in all the places where the traditional friendship of our families caused us to meet.

Together we shall agree upon a biography that is not prolix but is complete, simple but significant, which will outline him in his entirety, up to his glorious death; no words on his death, however, could be more effectual and moving than the letters which in merciful kindness you have communicated to me. I would think it a profanation to change them; and only those who have seen death with him can speak, have the right to speak, of his end.

The sea has helped me a great deal, helped physically, because my morale is always that of one in torment. I cannot speak of torment in the face of a grief like yours; I am afraid to draw on myself – and justly – the wrath and chastisement of Heaven.

Have courage, my poor dear; even if only out of a duty which is now sacred! Cultivate the memory.